CW00502021

The Evil Within

Alistair Birch

CITY STONE PUBLISHING

City Stone Publishing

ISBN (paperback): 978-1-915399-21-2
ISBN (ePUB): 978-1-915399-22-9

A CIP catalogue record for this book is available from the British Library.

Alistair Birch | www.alistairbirch.com

City Stone Publishing | www.citystonepublishing.com

June 2023

This book is dedicated to my wonderful wife,
Claire Birch x

Secrets are generally terrible. Beauty is not hidden, only ugliness and deformity.

L.M. Montgomery

Winter 1966

EMILY CLAY TRUDGED BACK toward the village. More snow had fallen and the wind bit, forcing the snow into high drifts. She wouldn't be crossing the fields tonight. Emily considered her position. She still had a mile to walk, and the road was treacherous. No chance of one of the local farmers driving by in the fading light, which was a shame, as her shoes offered no protection against the icy weather. It had been worth it, though. Another evening with *him*.

This time, they'd kissed. He had even let his hand wander over her breasts. Emily closed her eyes and walked on like an automaton as she savoured the memory. She'd experienced nothing like it. Boys her age were cloying idiots, all grease, odours, and fumbling. Tonight, he'd taken her to the cinema. He chose a western, *The Good, the Bad and the Ugly.* She didn't mind. She'd never been to a proper movie theatre, and she found the entire experience liberating. The film itself was boring, though she enjoyed the music with its funny sounding twangs. She didn't care. The film lasted for hours and that's why she'd gone along. For almost three hours, they'd sat together along a darkened row where other couples wrapped themselves together. And they did too.

Her foot slipped, breaking the spell, and Emily reminded herself she had to get home in one piece. The light had almost gone now, though she'd walked this road many times. The high hedges which fenced her in also stood as markers, so she couldn't stray away from the road. She felt tired. Poor fitness was her downfall, if only she'd bothered in PE class. No excuses. Once the weather cleared, she'd get more exercise. She had a boyfriend now and not just any school kid, a proper adult, so she would need to step up and make herself better for him. After all, she wanted to keep his interest.

Despite the conditions, Emily did a little skip. The action was a dumb move as her foot skidded off to the side upon landing and she lost control. A momentary realisation surfaced that she was going down with flailing arms, and then she felt her bottom land with a thump. A sting jabbed into her left ankle, along with a dull ache around her hips. The snow wasn't as soft as she'd hoped, though her gloves had saved her from some injury. She sat, momentarily dazed, as the numbness seeped into her bones.

The road was almost black now, and suddenly the village seemed a hundred miles away. Emily tried to stand, but immediately she fell back as a wave of pain travelled up her leg.

'Ouch,' she screamed before settling into silence once more. *Would someone hear her?* Sound normally travelled well across the fields, but the high hedges seemed to echo everything back and anyway, who'd be dumb enough to be out on a night like this?

Emily rolled onto her side and used her good leg to work into a kneeling position before attempting to stand. She got upright, but planting weight on her left foot wasn't good. More pain spikes came with each step. Now her neurosis joined in. *You're too fat. It's no wonder your foot hurts, the amount of weight you are putting down.*

She paused while the self-destructive thoughts flowed through her. It happened like this sometimes, but she knew the moment would pass. Her eyes glistened with tears, and she realised she couldn't stay put. Concentrating hard, Emily focussed on the white strip before her and limped on. She would not make any fuss, she was just going to get home and sneak up to her room unnoticed. Well, that was the plan, at least. She didn't have the strength to offer explanations to her parents.

Her stronger right foot stepped forward with a satisfying crunch, followed by a dragging sound as she pulled her opposite foot along. Another alien sound permeated the air. She stopped and cocked one ear. Whatever she thought she'd heard had stopped. She shook her head, more to convince herself she was being ridiculous than for warmth. She moved on. For a few steps, silence greeted her. It didn't last. The noise returned, closer now. A growl? No, more a guttural rasp. Her mind went into overdrive as she tried to speed up along the road. It was no good. The fierce jolts of pain forced her to settle into a weird hobble. She chanced a glance over her shoulder. Someone or something was there.

Emily faced forward again and ran. Or at least she tried. Any action was futile as her ankle buckled and she immediately collapsed. She landed hard, spluttering as a mouthful of snow lodged itself at the back of her throat, her arms unable to save her this time. Her brain became muddled as she crawled. The movement was slow and intensely cold. As she nudged forward, her mind taunted her. *Where had the shadowy figure gone?* She didn't want to know the answer. She desperately wanted to be home and snug more than ever.

Something gripped her sprained ankle, and Emily screamed. She attempted to roll onto her back, but it made no difference. Whatever had gripped her now twisted the joint, planting her face down into the snow. It was agony. She screamed again, but it was no good.

Her attacker reached over to thump the back of Emily's skull. Emily sensed the arm behind her, but was powerless to prevent what happened next. The first time her head pounded down, her face pushed through the snow and connected with the tarmac below. The pain was excruciating. Something grabbed a handful of hair and she felt herself being pulled upward. This was not the action of a saviour. After being lifted a few inches, her assailant rammed her head downwards for a second time.

An audible crunch of bone sounded out. Soon, Emily's body lay still.

Chapter One

Spring 1981

Mary Fortune was nothing like her name suggested. For starters, her family lived on a ramshackle farm where the dung filled outhouses looked disturbingly similar to the main farmhouse. Many of the neighbouring residents of Ascot Midden looked upon her family with disdain. Their unkempt appearance jarred against the thriving community. Despite this and the fact the girl was unerringly quiet, most of the villagers saw Mary as harmless.

'Hi Mary. What are you doing down here?'

The voice came from Phil Riley, who ran the village shop. He smiled warmly, as he did with most of his customers. Mary looked on mute before pointing nervously at a stack of fresh bread.

The shopkeeper reached down and selected the loaf. He continued his gentle chit chat, but each time her response remained the same as her lips remained closed. Instead, only her finger moved from shelf to shelf. The only time he noticed any flicker of emotion was when he asked about her brother. The girl's eyes cast downward, which showed Phil she wasn't about to share. Instead, she continued to point at other groceries until she'd filled her wicker basket. Soon, the girl handed over her money and exited the shop without offering a word. Phil shrugged. It didn't matter. Mary's money was as good as anyone's. Her mind just worked a little differently to others.

Keith Fortune looked on as his young sister walked away. She struggled with her bulging basket, but he made no move to help her. Even when she started up the long steep drag to home, he held back. Instead, he lazed upon a bench beside the church, enjoying the sun. Stretching his powerful arms behind his head, he let out an enormous yawn as he allowed the sunshine to envelop him. The warmth was inviting, and he soon forgot about his sister's woes.

An hour later, the sun had shifted and Keith finally found his seat cast into shadow. He stood, kicked over a few daffodils, and headed for home. The walk took him just ten minutes as he cut across the fields. Mary's journey had taken twenty.

Once he'd reached their farm, he headed across the filthy yard and walked straight into the kitchen. Mary was inside, scrubbing the floor. She looked uncomfortable as her knees pressed down hard on the floor tiles.

Keith gave her a disdainful glare. 'Did you buy everything?'

She nodded before dipping her head to focus on scrubbing harder. Keith walked across to inspect her work. He stepped away, leaving a trail of dung and mud behind.

'You missed a bit,' he chuckled as he carved a doorstep slice off the loaf and paired it with a huge wedge of cheese. Satisfied, he moved off upstairs, where he could settle and have another snooze.

Chapter Two

Summer 1981

THE SUN WAS BEATING down hard as Stuart Lockwood raced down the bridle path. In the distance, he could see the shape of Paul Winters. His friend would soon be a speck unless he could pick up some pace. Paul wouldn't ease up, but then Stuart knew that. The sixteen-year-olds were friends; Paul was taller and stronger, traits he loved to brag about. The summer holidays were only a few days old, and neither boy would watch the calendar to see when they had to return to school. Life was good.

Stuart's breath came in sharp bursts now as the path stretched out ahead. He was running too fast for comfort. Any casual observer would see fear etched into the boy's features as he hurtled down the path with spindly arms windmilling through the air. For a moment, it appeared he would fall as the slope angled down sharply. Leaving a dust cloud behind, he finally hit tarmac where the path flattened out, allowing him to slow. Ahead, beyond the farmhouse, stood the woodland path where Paul had disappeared a minute earlier.

He caught his breath, which came in loud rasps, and clutched a wall for support. Stuart wretched, but Paul had disappeared into the undergrowth so he pushed off again, leaving a sweaty palm print in his wake. The path through the trail was much darker and after tripping over a tree root, he slowed to a walk. That was, until he heard shouts from the field ahead.

Exiting the tree line, Stuart blew out his cheeks before letting loose a chuckle as he mounted the wooden fence. Ahead, his friend charged around the field, whooping with laughter while sending sheep scattering in all directions. Wiping his arm across his brow, he smeared sweat across his t-shirt before climbing down. It was time to have some fun.

'Oi, you let them get away,' Stuart chided, as an agile sheep twisted away from Paul's outstretched grasp.

'Well, come on then, get your bum over here and help me.'

There were around forty sheep in the field, but no matter how hard the pair tried, they were no match for the animals. Eventually Stuart collapsed by a nearby stream, where he splashed his face with the icy water. He bent closer to the brook and scooped water, which he launched towards Paul. The cascade landed, and his friend took retribution by storming at him, causing Stuart to fall over into the water.

He appeared, elated by the refreshing crystal waters. Straight away he knew he must return to battle. Taking care, he stood and once his feet had solid purchase; he faced Paul and tried to throw him into the water. Paul wavered for a minute before he lost balance. Coming up for air and soaking wet, he grinned as he stepped out of the water.

'I think we'll call that one a draw,' Stuart offered, knowing very well he'd taken more hits.

'You reckon? I suppose so,' Paul conceded. Across the grass, the flock of sheep eyed them warily. None were keen to approach.

Stuart studied his friend's intense expression. *Why did he look angry?*

Whatever the mood he thought he saw, it vanished in an instant. Stuart decided it must have been his imagination.

'So, what shall we do next?' he queried.

Paul remained silent, so Stuart followed his gaze until both were staring at a lone sheep. He thought they'd finished with livestock chasing, especially as Paul stood and headed back to the tree line. Stuart got up to follow, but any thought they were heading home vanished when his friend returned a minute later, carrying two sturdy branches. He tossed one down before wielding his own weapon like a light sabre. Paul embellished the movement with a weird swishing sound.

'Come on,' he called as he raced across towards the field toward the stranded ovine.

Stuart stood and reluctantly picked up the branch. His stick was smaller than Paul's, and he only wanted to use the weapon to corral the animal and force it along their chosen path, but Paul had other ideas. In the several seconds it took him to cross the field, Paul had closed the gap to the animal. The sheep looked skittish as it ran left and then right, but each time Paul beat down and forced the animal back. This was wrong. Stuart felt conflict raging as he stood alongside his friend. A pair of black slits marked the animal's eyes, which shook from side to side as hooves pounded the dirt.

Both boys closed in, with Paul taking an aggressive stance. His arms waved the branch, mimicking a samurai. He was closest and caused the sheep to take flight. The animal tried to squeeze into the hedge when Paul speared his branch down, grazing the side of the animal's head. The sheep bleated in distress before retreating.

Stuart looked on in disbelief. *Had he just seen his best friend try to cave in a sheep's skull?*

Everything was a noisy blur. Suddenly, the woolly animal charged toward Stuart, who faltered and stepped back. The gap which formed was enough, and the sheep wriggled through.

'You idiot,' Paul shouted. 'Why'd you let it get away?'

Stuart sank down. The wretched feeling he'd felt during the run returned, only this time the mood paired with guilt. Stuart wavered in response before throwing the branch down and heading towards the gate. Once there, he paused and took stock. *Paul was his friend. Not that bad, was it? Just high spirits, that's all.* Stuart didn't like being called an idiot, but earlier in the afternoon had been fun.

'Sorry, it was quicker than I expected. Come on, there are a few clouds in the sky now. Let's head home.'

A rope looped across the gate post. Stuart gripped the rough tethering and lifted, allowing them to leave the field. Once we they were outside, he tugged the gate closed.

'What are you doing?' Paul grumbled.

'Erm, tying up the gate,' Stuart responded nervously.

'Leave it open,' Paul commanded.

'Come on, Paul, we've had our fun.' He could feel his face reddening as he raised the rope to drop it over a post to hold the gate shut.

Paul stepped forward and jerked the rope free before kicking a wooden slat until the gate swung wide again. He still held his branch, which he tapped into one fist as though the kick wasn't intimidating enough.

Stuart didn't want any drama, though the day had taken a downward turn outside of his control. *They were friends. He wouldn't hurt me, would he?* He knew their attack on the sheep had gone too far and they'd be in trouble if anyone had seen. Stuart turned and grabbed the gate, pulling it closed again. The rope felt coarse in his sweaty hands as he draped it back over the post.

'Let's go,' he said sternly, pushing on along the path. Suddenly, he lurched backwards as Paul grabbed his elbow before he could pass.

'I was right. You are an idiot,' Paul taunted. With that, he threw his branch to one side and reached into his jeans. He extracted a pen knife and took a few seconds as he clumsily opened the blade he needed. It glinted in the sunshine, and his face took on the same frenzied appearance Stuart had seen earlier. Although the rope was thick, it was also old, and after less than a minute of sawing, Paul let out a cheer. He levelled several kicks and even splintered one of the thinner struts. The gate yawed wide with nothing to hold it shut.

Stuart's heart sank as he looked on in frightened exasperation, but there was nothing he could do. Paul strode past triumphantly, off into the woods.

'You coming?' he asked when he reached the first tree.

Stuart looked at the mess behind in dismay. Suddenly, he didn't want to be there anymore. Meekly, he turned and followed into the shade.

The walk back from the field was quiet, but once they were closer to home, conversation warmed again as the pair chatted about the water fight. They were best friends, and the idea of losing Paul meant Stuart quickly forgave and forgot.

Later the same day, Stuart didn't think twice, when Paul encouraged him to pinch washing from Mrs Mather's line. The idea seemed innocent enough. Yet as soon as he faced an enormous pair of knickers twice the size of his head, he felt foolish. *Why on earth am I doing this?* Mrs Mather was old enough to be his gran. His hand wavered as he reached up, ready to snatch the garment down and sprint to safety.

An angry shout ruptured the game. 'What are you doing, boy?'

Stuart withdrew his arm as though someone had struck him. He looked left and right, but the swirling sheets conspired to block his view. Outside of the garden, all he could hear was Paul's laughter. He abandoned all attempts at thievery. Better to run away where his friend would mock than risk capture. Deciding the voice must have come from the cottage, he ran toward the gate at the bottom of the garden. Seconds later he'd spilled out and was speeding up, away to his friend.

'You jammy git,' Paul said once they were both in the clear.

Stuart's chest was heaving, and it took him a few seconds to reply. 'Bloody hell. I'm not going back in there in a hurry.'

'You'd better. A deal is a deal,' Paul taunted.

Stuart thought for a moment. 'Maybe another time,' he offered, hoping his friend would forget in a day or two.

The rest of the afternoon went without incident. Stuart headed for home, with Paul doing likewise.

As soon as he walked through the front door, Stuart knew something was amiss. He could hear his parents in the living room, deep in conversation. He paused in the hallway, trying to decide whether to head for the safety of his bedroom, or stay put and listen in. While he dithered, they took away the decision from him as he saw his mother standing in the doorway.

'Come in, we want to talk to you.' Her command left no room to manoeuvre.

Stuart meekly followed. He was sure the owner of the shouting voice from the garden must have paid a visit, so he readied himself for questioning.

She directed him to the sofa before returning to drape an arm across the imposing figure of his dad, who sat in an armchair opposite. Stuart wanted to be anywhere except there.

'Have you been anywhere near Hunter Field recently?' It was his father who spoke first.

The question completely wrongfooted him. The delay in answering probably looked guilty, but there was nothing Stuart could do. In the end, he settled for a vigorous shake of the head, whilst remaining silent. He could see his dad's eyes boring into him, trying to extract the truth. In the end, his father appeared to give up.

Stuart sat there, wondering if it was safe to get up and head for his room. In the end, curiosity got the better of him. 'So, what happened at Hunter Field?' he asked quietly.

'Some bastard destroyed a gate and let most of the sheep loose. Half the flock made it out onto the main road.'

Hearing his dad swear was an unfamiliar experience. He should have foreseen the answer which had come, but shock showed across his face. Stuart felt certain his cheeks must be flushing. He looked left and right, keen to get out of the room, but it would not be that easy. As he waited to see if they would excuse him, he asked another question. 'What happened to them?'

Stuart's father seemed to age before him as he replied. 'They rounded most up, but not before an accident happened.'

Stuart's chest tightened as he waited for his dad to continue.

'There was a two car pile up when the sheep ran out into the road,' came the flat response.

Stuart felt sick. Knowing they were to blame was too much to bear. He could think of no way he could make amends. In the end, he sat in silence. The mood became awkward as Stuart waited, keen to leave or to hear the outcome of the accident. At first, neither parent offered resolution until his mother patted her husband on the shoulder and moved away to the kitchen. Stuart looked down to avoid eye contact before gingerly standing and walking out of the room. He knew he looked guilty. For now, at least, it seemed he'd got away with one.

The next day, Stuart walked through the village and up along Westcot Lane, expecting to see Paul, but there was no sign. Even when he knocked on their front door, nobody came. Their house stood empty.

Stuart turned to head back down the hill, wondering where his friend had gone to.

Chapter Three

September 1981

DESPITE THE POUNDING RAIN, the pupils of Chancery School stood in four orderly lines as they waited to be sorted into their respective classes for the new year. The lucky ones bunched up at the back of each line as they sought shelter near the wall behind. Everyone else looked on morosely as they became drenched.

Founded when Henry the Eighth was on the throne, the all boys' school stood for traditional standards, despite being a lot newer than many of the nearby colleges within Oxfordshire. The school sat to the south of the county, though heads and governors alike, attached themselves to the Oxford name, content to bask in ill deserved kudos.

The school had successfully survived World War II, only to be burned down in the late nineteen forties. The governors chose a new site, yet the architects and a lack of funds combined resulted in a new school which appeared to most as a post-war monstrosity. A long two-storey row of grey classrooms made up most of the building, with a section at one end for the great hall and gymnasium. Viewed from above, the entire structure resembled an axe. The dull aspect was only one part of the change, which would have left the founder, Ernest Whitfield, turning in his grave. By the early sixties, they made a major change by admitting girls to their ranks.

Roger Daley coughed as he looked out of the window at the rabble below. If the previous year were anything to go by, then this would be another tough year. The teacher watched through narrowed eyes as two colleagues wrestled with their protective umbrellas in the gusty wind while Craig Simmons, the head of year, read names off a clipboard. The scene was a mess, and Daley wondered why they didn't just open up the gymnasium to complete the students' enrolment. Barry Potts and Arthur Morgan were the reason, Daley surmised. As the head of PE and the school caretaker respectively, they made for a formidable pair. It was a shame for everyone outside, as Mr Simmons showed reluctance to force everyone inside. Daley coughed again, frustrated he couldn't dip outside for a cigarette or, better still, smoke inside.

At long last, the pupils appeared to be sorted and the staff ushered the children inside. Daley descended a set of stone steps, choosing to pause halfway down. He tutted as he took in the chaotic scene ahead. The hall was too small for over one hundred pupils to stay within their allotted lines, and immediately, the rank and order disintegrated until a solid mass of children formed. Simmons came in last. The man struggled to close the umbrella, in the end choose an awkward pose where the clipboard wedged between both knees. The move was unsuccessful as the umbrella clattered to the floor. Daley chuckled.

'There you are, Daley.' The voice came from Susan Rutt. Her voice was shrill, which helped to quell the clamouring children who swarmed around her.

In private, Daley would have called his colleague "Runt", but not today. He planted a fake smile before bellowing, 'Silence!'

A hush descended. Everyone, including his colleagues, succumbed. He directed his focus on the children. 'Right, I can see you are all soaked. Those of you in class B4 need to follow me.' Daley turned and climbed the stairs. Once he reached the first floor, he cast a backward glance. As expected, his command succeeded as a quarter of the children broke away and began the climb. He led the rabble along the first-floor corridor and into his classroom, where he waited at the front. The students shuffled into the room and stood in a long line which meandered across the room. Daley offered an icy stare, which soon calmed their chatter. A few kids returned the same withering appraisals, which Daley noted, but considering they were all soaked, it seemed they were well enough behaved.

Daley sat and wrapped his warm palms together as he faced his students, who stood shivering before him. The teacher had already turned off the radiators in his classroom, reasoning he wasn't stupid enough to stand in the rain, so the children should suffer for their ineptitude. It was irrelevant. This choice hadn't been theirs to make. Daley seemed happy enough to set his entire class upon a path of dislike against the foolish staff who'd caused their soggy discomfort.

For the next half hour, he sorted the fourth-year secondary-grade pupils alphabetically, which left Stuart Lockwood seated in the middle and Paul Winters in the far-right corner. Daley handed workbooks and assignments out. It didn't bother him he hadn't taught the new intake yet. He wanted to start the year how he meant to go on by pushing these kids hard, and for today that meant a test. At first there were murmurs of discontent, which Daley soon quashed with a mix of threats and kindness. The threats were a simple exploration so Daley could identify which children would rebel, and within the first few minutes, he'd made some notes on who he should watch. The kindness was fake. He'd told the class that if they behaved properly for the morning sessions, he'd investigate getting the heating turned up, an act he had no intention of following through.

He looked on from the comfort of his chair. Sixteen boys and thirteen girls sat before him. Most were scribbling furiously, as expected. Several stared about, mainly through the window. By the time the bell approached, Daley felt he had a measure of the children in his form group. There were a few who showed potential. Not as excellent students, he hardly cared for their wellbeing, but as youngsters he could exploit.

Daley considered that this year's intake could be fun after all.

It was only the first class of the year, even so, it dragged on. Paul Winters was already wondering how he could skip school. Being sat in the corner, tucked in at the back of the class, suited him just fine, though the single pane glass offered no comfort as he'd shivered with droplets of water pooling around his feet. Being separated from Stuart was another black mark. What was that about? In juniors and even during the first years of secondary, the pair had been inseparable and, apart from the odd occasion when a teacher had sent him to stand in the corridor; he had free rein to muck about as he pleased.

When the class had started, he'd examined the written test they gave him with contempt. There were thirty questions. With sorting out timetables and other admin, that left just forty minutes in the double period left to complete. The test comprising maths questions, none of which were difficult. This amused Paul. There was no way he would advertise he knew what he was doing. Instead, he answered the first three sums using an awful scrawl and then turned his attention to draw random doodles which spanned the remaining paper. He looked across towards his friend, though like the other students, Stuart had his head down and appeared to be working. That left two things for Paul to study: the world outside and Mr Daley, who slouched in relaxed comfort at the front of the room. It was the first time in his classroom but he recognised the teacher and had witnessed just how he behaved towards his pupils. Outside, the weather was wild. Paul found it attractive. It didn't matter that the clouds were slate grey as rain pelted down, though even he would have sought shelter in preference to the stupid act of lining up in a downpour. For now, the school had him trapped, so he tore his eyes away from the outside gloom and studied Mr Daley. The pair briefly locked eyes together and then the bell sounded, breaking the spell. Paul and the others stood immediately.

'Sit back down,' their new form teacher barked. Most complied, immediately lowering their backsides, but not Paul nor one other newcomer to the class. They stood at opposing sides of the classroom, each glaring toward their teacher. Finally, the ringing came to an abrupt end as the entire class looked on with renewed interest. Outside, the corridor seemed to erupt in a clamour of footsteps and accompanying chatter.

Daley consulted his register. 'Winters, Blake, I gave you both an instruction. Sit!'

The boy identified as Blake flushed before lowering himself into his seat, but Paul remained standing. Instead of complying, Paul grinned and then looked out of the window with a bored expression on his face.

'As you wish. Everyone, when you look for someone to blame for your lack of break time, make sure you blame Winters here.'

Paul shrugged; inside, he was fuming. He didn't care to miss out on a break, especially while it was pissing down outside, but punishing his classmates would make some enemies on the first day. Reluctantly, he offered contrition.

'Sorry, sir,' he said as he lowered himself onto the seat.

The noise outside remained, as a mix of grumpy and excited pupils ambled toward the great hall, rather than head outside into the downpour. Inside the classroom, everybody was silent. Paul looked around, conscious of the all the eyes staring in his direction. His expectation for the class to clear now he'd complied wasn't happening. He lowered his eyes. Suddenly, he didn't want to be there anymore. Despite the stone cold radiators, Paul felt hot under his teacher's gaze. The days when he was the tallest and biggest in the junior school seemed a distant memory. Now instead, he sat in a burgundy blazer two sizes too big, with a tie which sought to strangle him. He cast a glance up and instantly regretted it. His new form tutor was looming over him, with eyes ablaze. The withering stare continued as the entire class looked on. To Paul, it appeared time had slowed. Even the raindrops which meandered down the window panes seemed leisurely in their descent. Paul cast a glance at his watch. Somehow, it had been fully five minutes since the bell had sounded, a third of their break time.

'Right, everyone outside,' Daley commanded. 'Not you, Winters,' he continued as he pressed down onto Paul's shoulder, forcing him back into his seat. The physical contact made Paul feel uncomfortable, and he sank lower until his teacher lifted his palm away.

Paul looked on morosely as the classroom cleared. As if to compound his mood, Daley strolled over and closed the door. Daley returned to the front of the classroom and settled down, choosing to rest his elbows on a table and his chin on his palms. With everyone's departure, the rain seemed suddenly louder. Paul waited, unsure what was to come.

'I was like you, at your age,' Daley began. 'A jumped up little tosser.'

Paul bridled at the comment, though he had no response. Certainly, none of the teachers in his previous school would have ever spoken to him in that manner. He considered his position. Day one in a new school, being called out and insulted by his new teacher. Not an impressive start. But then, did he care? In a rare show of restraint, Paul listened.

'Good. It's about time you paid attention,' said Daley, who'd clearly noticed Winters shift. 'Here is what I expect from you. This year and every year you remain at this school, you have my permission to dick around in class.'

Paul's eyes knitted together as he tried to process the instruction. This wasn't what he'd expected at all, and the idea completely threw him. 'Sir?' was all he could meekly offer.

'Look, I see your type all the time. Lazy, worthless wankers who actually have potential. I know you are going to arse about, and that's fine. I couldn't care less as long as you do as I say.'

The heat which Paul had felt earlier returned. He had just been told he could muck about in class! He couldn't comprehend his new status, but one word formed in his mind. *Legend.*

It was lunchtime before Paul got to speak with Stuart properly. The rain had eased to a drizzle and puddles pooled across the playground. The sixth-formers had grabbed the best shelters, but the pair had cowered underneath a weeping willow near the hockey pitch.

'Bloody hell, Paul. You started strong by pissing Daley off first chance you got, didn't you?'

Paul smiled. Already he was basking under the guise of a rebel. 'What about you, though? You seemed to do the opposite. Teacher's pet or what?'

Stuart raised both hands in mock submission. 'Come off it. Today's our first day. I didn't know what to do and anyway, the entire class sat down when the bell went and he started shouting at us.'

'Tosser,' Paul called, dipping into the new vocabulary Daley had taught him.

'Yeah, I guess so. How old is he, Daley I mean?'

Paul considered the question before offering a throwaway figure of a hundred. They both laughed.

'Who was the other kid?' Stuart continued. 'You know, the one who stayed standing like you, Blake, was it?'

Paul thought. With so many unfamiliar faces, many of whom sat between him and this new kid, he wasn't sure. It was too early to say if there was any potential for an alliance. There were only four children who'd come up to Chancery's from the tiny primary school in their village of Ascot Midden. Along with Paul and Stuart were Mary Fortune and Liam Pratt. Paul had watched Mary and Liam during their first years of secondary and deemed both as worthless, except as targets for his amusement.

'Come on,' Paul commanded. 'Let's find out if Blake or whatever he's called is worth getting to know.'

It turned out that Blake was indeed worth getting to know. Sure, he'd meekly obeyed when Daley had confronted him, but Paul could see a kindred spirit when he saw one, though he failed to notice the hint of jealousy etched across Stuart's face.

Chapter Four

December 1981

THE FIRST SCHOOL TERM had been a blast for Paul Winters and Stuart Lockwood. Even Harry Blake seemed to have settled as a welcome member of their gang, though it suited Stuart that Harry lived in the opposite direction from Ascot Midden. Having Paul's undivided attention on the school bus journeys helped him keep top spot as the best friend. Today was a special day, the end of the term and the start of the Christmas holidays.

Stuart looked at Paul while Mr Daley took the classroom register. Outside, a hard frost gripped the windows. But unlike their first day, now at least two radiators offered token warmth. Not for Stuart, though. His place, stuck in the middle of the class, left him shivering. Paul snapped back to attention as Mr Daley called his name. He responded with his usual dull sounding, 'Sir,' before wrapping his arms about his torso. There had to be a law about keeping kids in such a cold classroom. Across the room, Blake sniggered as he mockingly pressed his palms upon the radiator, mimicking a concert pianist. There was only one saving grace. Within their other classes, the trio could choose where to sit, as long as they weren't too disruptive. He checked his watch. Just five minutes until break time and then he could escape the classroom fridge until the new year.

Without warning, Daley slapped a hefty textbook down on his desk with a loud thump. It broke everyone's chatter.

'Now that I have everyone's attention,' Daley continued, 'there is just time for me to pass on my traditional Christmas present.'

A flurry of voices greeted their tutor's comment before being silenced, as Daley thudded the textbook for a second time. Stuart glanced at his friends in doubtful expectation. Upon seeing their confused expressions, he turned to the front again to see Daley handing papers to the front row of students. They passed the sheets back until everyone had a copy. There were four sides of A4, the first of which was titled, "Christmas Questionnaire".

Stuart's mood sank as he turned over the cover. Inside were lots of questions. He browsed through them, counting one hundred. He remembered the maths test for the class at the beginning of term, but this was completely different. Each question seemed odd. Question one: name all the churches in Oxford with St Mary in the name. The rest followed in a similar vein, with questions ranging from William Morris through to J. R. R. Tolkien.

'Good,' Daley cheered, with an enthusiasm which seemed absent from the pupils. 'You might think you know it all since you've been at school for a couple of years but I have a traditional gift to all who come into my class for the first time. I don't care if you think this is a junior assignment, I'm demanding it from you.' He looked stern. 'You'll need to be out and about during the holiday, gathering the answers. Make sure you answer *every* question without exception. Those of you with older siblings can ask them what happened to the ones who didn't bother.'

With those parting words, the bell sounded and for once Daley allowed his class to disperse without comment.

'Shit, have you seen the size of this thing?' Stuart said once they were clear of the throng. 'How the hell are we going to get all this information?'

A week later, Stuart and Paul climbed off the bus at Carfax, Oxford. Pedestrians swarmed around as the pair fought their way along Queen Street and down towards the Westgate Centre.

'Why are we even bothering?' Paul asked in disgust. 'Come on, there's no way we're going to answer all of Daley's questions.'

'Yeh, I know, but we've got to do something, haven't we? And, anyway, the village is dead at the moment. There's nothing going on, so why not have a mooch about town?'

'Suppose,' Paul conceded.

Together, they approached Bonn Square. Street vendors offered food and Oxford branded hats and scarves, while merry Christmas music piped in the background. All of this was in stark contrast to the clutch of down and outs who forlornly huddled in damp blankets on icy stone steps. Paul looked on in disgust. 'If I ever end up like that, shoot me,' he chided.

'You already look like them,' Stuart retorted bravely, resulting in an elbow to the gut. Paul's eyes narrowed, as he headed for the shopping mall. The move took them away from the cold air but served little other purpose. They stopped outside a chocolate shop and stared longingly through the window at the expensive sweets inside. Keeping away from the doorway, Stuart pulled out the questionnaire and thrust it under his friend's nose. 'So, where do we start?'

Paul looked at the crumpled paper before returning a scathing look. 'You can do the bloody thing if you like. I can't be arsed.'

The response was no surprise, but frustrated Stuart all the same. He didn't want to do the work either, though felt he had to show some effort at least. Sighing forlornly, he read the first question for the umpteenth time. The action did him no favours. Just as he went to tuck the paper away, Paul tugged him roughly on his elbow.

'Look who it is?' he said while pointing through the crowd.

Ahead, some fifty yards away, was Mary Fortune. She stood out among the shoppers. Whether it was the cold or the surging crowds, her diminutive figure shrank back against a shop window whenever people came too close. Stuart looked on, torn. He could already work out what Paul was thinking. It didn't sit well.

'Why are you staring? Do you fancy her or something?' Paul joked, snapping Stuart's attention back to the present.

'Don't be dumb,' he replied unconvincingly.

'Christ. You bloody do. Ha, my mate's got the hots for the village mouse. Wait until Harry hears this.'

'I do *not*, idiot. You pointed her out, and I looked, that's all.'

'Prove it then,' Paul challenged.

Stuart's insides lurched and suddenly the questionnaire seemed a distant memory. As his mind scrambled, shoppers in the crowd surged forward, buffeting the boys into the nearest shop doorway. It took a few seconds of shoving before the pair broke free, by which time Mary had vanished.

'So, what do we do now?' Stuart shouted above the clamour.

Paul ignored him, choosing instead to scour the area, intent upon finding the girl. Seeing she'd disappeared, he swore and punched his fist against the nearest shop window.

For the next hour, Stuart wandered the streets of Oxford with Paul dragging along behind. On the surface, neither seemed to have any direction or aim for their nomadic wandering, though both were wondering whether they'd bump into Mary again.

'Come on, I'm getting cold. Let's hop in here,' Stuart groaned, while pointing at the Museum of Oxford.

Paul swallowed back a can of coke and belched loudly. Gripping the empty tin, he twisted it firmly until the metal container became a crushed, ripped mess which he threw upon the pavement. 'Alright, got to be better than walking around this dump.'

Stuart cringed. He desperately wanted to pick up the can and place it in the nearest bin, but he could feel Paul's eyes drilling into him. He knew there was an unspoken challenge. Stuart kicked the tin to the relative safety of the edge of the pavement before turning to mount the steps and push through the museum's door.

Inside, the world was completely different. The entrance appeared empty apart from a solitary tour guide, who greeted him enthusiastically. 'Welcome to the Museum of Oxford. What can I do for you this fine December day?' the overweight character in a dark red cardigan several sizes too big boomed.

The boys looked at one another, dumbfounded. The weather certainly wasn't fine and the joviality which greeted them felt alien. Stuart looked about as Paul turned to leave.

Ignoring the awkward silence, the man persisted, 'I bet you're here for the Alice in Wonderland exhibit. Ah, yes, a wonderful display. It is very interesting, as you'll see. Just head along the corridor and down the stairs at the end.'

Something nudged the pair in the back. They were blocking the entrance as a family crowded through. Stuart offered an embarrassed smile as he walked off down the corridor. A few steps on, he cut a backward glance. Paul was following, his face a mask of anger. Upon reaching the steps, Stuart slowed.

'What the hell are we doing in here?' Paul demanded. 'Come on, I'm not sticking around in this freak show.'

Stuart paused.

'Well? What are you waiting for?' Paul's command left little room for doubt, but Stuart remained rooted on the top step, his hand whitening as he gripped the rail.

'Suit yourself, bloody idiot,' Paul grumbled, before marching back to the entrance hall.

Seconds later, Stuart heard a solid thud as his friend slammed the outer door, to the dismay of the lobby guide. Stuart sighed. He reached into his pocket to extract the assignment. It felt odd to be away from Paul, though after months of tormenting smaller classmates, the newly found solitude came as a relief.

The stairs were gloomy, but Stuart strode purposefully down until he reached the exhibit he was looking for. He turned left, hoping to find some answers for his assignment, when the sight of Mary stopped him in his tracks. She was across the room, studying a display, and she hadn't seen him. The tightness which had gripped his hand on the rail earlier now moved to his chest as he felt his breathing quicken. He stood, transfixed. Paul had been right. He *did* have a crush on Mary. And now an opportunity had presented itself. All the bravado, frequently coupled with aggression in the playground as part of Paul's gang, evaporated on the spot.

He couldn't breathe properly as his hands, slick with sweat, flailed hopelessly to pull the door shut before she could turn around. This was ridiculous. He had a reputation. Well, no, not really. He was just a bumbling third year. It was Paul who had a reputation, but Stuart had tagged himself and by extension he was someone others feared. Did Mary fear him? The mere thought sent a shiver across his back. That wasn't at all what he wanted. Conflicting, panic filled thoughts flowed through his brain, leaving him standing mute and confused. Floundering, Stuart stared down at his questionnaire as though the sheets of paper would magically offer some answers.

He risked a glance upward and immediately wished he hadn't. She was staring at him. No, *through* him. Stuart's eyes glazed over, and he was sure he'd let out a little whimper. Her eyes didn't seem to waver, and Stuart was sure he looked like a gibbering idiot. Still, her stare persisted. This was crazy. Stuart wanted to look into her beautiful brown eyes while holding her hands. He shook himself and looked in dismay as his papers fluttered downwards to settle upon the floor. She offered the merest hint of a smile.

Stuart bent down to sweep up the sheets. Had he imagined it? Was there warmth or mockery? He couldn't tell, but the knotting within his belly made the return to a standing position difficult. Now a fresh problem surfaced as he felt heat rising across his neck and upward until his entire face seemed to be caught in a blaze. Surely she could see his discomfort, but no, she'd turned away, back to her studies.

For the first time, Stuart appraised the room properly. Apart from Mary, there was no one else. Glass display cabinets lined the wall nearest the door, with four more filling the middle of the room. At the far end stood a partition, though no sounds issued, confirming Stuart's assessment it was just the two of them there. He moved forward with heavy legs until he found himself alongside her.

She was staring at a pamphlet.

'What are you reading?' Stuart blurted, feeling awkward.

Mary tilted her head, revealing an angelic face with high cheekbones. Stuart savoured the delicious sight. Even the image of her lips talking seemed to captivate. Her reply went unheard in Stuart's haze. 'Sorry, what did you just say?' he asked.

Mary's face hardened before gesturing to a pile of leaflets near the door. 'The story is quite interesting, really. It's all about the inspiration for *Alice in Wonderland*. I've already answered a couple of our Christmas questions.'

'Wow. Can I see?'

Mary's smile faltered. 'Is he with you?'

'Who?' Stuart asked, before cursing himself for realising the obvious. 'Sorry, no, he's gone off somewhere,' he recovered.

'Good. You shouldn't hang around with him. He's trouble.'

Her insight was spot on. But coming from a girl who had always been so quiet, it came as a shock.

'I guess,' was all he could muster.

She shrugged, thrusting the pamphlet under his nose.

'Here, read this', she suggested.

Stuart nodded weakly, confused by how different she was from her usual quiet behaviour, as if she'd come to life. He soon saw she'd been right. One question on their assignment referred to *Alice in Wonderland*. It wanted to know the middle name of the girl upon which Lewis Carroll had based the book. There, typed before them both, was the answer, Alice Pleasance Liddell. Feeling uncharted emotions, Stuart took a chance.

'Would you mind if I worked with you on our assignment?'

There, he'd asked. She could only say no. She would say no, right? Only she didn't.

Chapter Five

January 1982

MARY FORTUNE CONGRATULATED HERSELF. She couldn't believe just how well the Christmas holiday had gone. Well, that wasn't entirely true. Her life on the farm remained a stagnant torture of domestic drudgery, but she'd talked to Stuart. That breakthrough was something she'd dreamed about, even before they moved up to Chancery's. She knew Stuart was rough around the edges, but put that down to the company he kept. A bitter taste sat on her lips as she considered Paul and the other crony Harry. Stuart showed no signs of moving away from that clique, which hampered all her attempts to get closer to him. Still, they'd spent a few wonderful hours in Oxford together, and for the briefest of times, she'd felt normal. She clung to that feeling. She *had* to.

'What are you gawping at?'

Keith's fiercely rasping question cut through Mary's daydream. Dumbly, she shook her head and turned away to collect the breakfast dishes. She hadn't eaten, yet as always, she'd prepared a huge breakfast for Keith and her parents. That was a joke. Her mother barely ate and, as for her father, he wouldn't have sobered up enough to eat yet. Her generous plate of bacon and eggs accompanied by sausages and toast would go in the bin. But most likely, Keith wouldn't let it go to waste. No wonder his body had taken on the shape of a barrel. Looking down, as she always did at home, Mary scrubbed the pan harder. She needed to be abrasive to remove all the hardened greasy bacon, but she also needed an outlet for her frustrations. Keith barged into her and the pan clanged loudly in the basin, causing soap suds to splash across the drainer and down Mary's top.

'I said, what are you gawping at?' Her brother grabbed her elbow in a vicious grip and spun her around.

She stifled a cry of pain as she looked down, avoiding his eyes. She couldn't let her eyes meet his. That would be a certain route to more abuse. Instead, she retreated to her meek and quiet defence. Subservience, another bitter pill to swallow. 'I was just checking to see if you'd eaten enough breakfast, as I wanted to get everything washed away before leaving for school.'

The grip slackened as Keith patted his vast belly. She could see him eyeing up the second plate, left out for their father.

'You know what? Since I do all the work around here, I think I deserve to eat Dad's plate. You'd best dry that pan and set another pile of bacon cooking. You won't want him to come down to no breakfast now, would you?'

Mary buckled inwardly. She'd miss the school bus if she stayed to cook a second breakfast. The school and her teachers wouldn't understand if she turned up an hour late because she had to walk the three miles. She knew the unfairness of the situation, yet Keith's towering form left her no choice. As the grip on her arm finally released, Mary dried the frying pan and set it back atop the stove.

Chapter Six

April 1982

THE MONTHS HAD FLOWN by in a whirl of confusing emotions. Stuart found himself constantly on edge. He'd completed the Christmas assignment satisfactorily, much to his joyful surprise, and his friendship with Mary showed signs of blossoming. They set all of this excitement against a hefty backdrop of secrecy. Paul seemed to strengthen his position as a bully, aided by Harry Blake, who'd grown into the role of enforcer. With each passing day, Stuart felt more like an outcast.

Today he sniffed noisily as he tried to inhale snot back upwards into his left nostril. It was a futile action, and he soon wiped the excess across his cuff.

'Where is this sodding place again?' he moaned.

'Come on, you dick, don't you ever listen? Cherrytree Animal Reserve, or some shit like that,' Paul responded.

Stuart snorted. 'Christ, you don't even know where we're going. Not just me who wasn't listening then.'

'Can it, Lockwood,' Daley growled as he shoved the pair further along the bus. The boys moved silently down the aisle, with Paul keeping his lunch bag at shoulder height to whack as many heads along the way as possible. Together, they sprawled across the five seats at the rear until Harry finally arrived, grabbing the middle pew. Harry ignored Stuart as he planted his bulk across the middle.

'Hey, I am here, you know,' Stuart sniffled.

'Oh, yeah. I didn't see you down there, Stu,' came Harry's arrogant reply.

Paul guffawed. 'Get a room, you two.'

Stuart wrestled himself out from underneath Harry and slouched to one side, stealthily smearing a snotty palm across his friend. Harry's back now resembled a slug trail, but Stuart didn't care. It was payback for his incursion. The rest of the journey went without incident, though Paul and Harry both spent their time chewing up clumps of paper in readiness to throw at unwitting pupils further down the bus. Each soggy splat resulted in an outraged child turning, only to be greeted by a trio of grinning idiots in the back row. Stuart took part, but he threw far fewer missiles, and he cringed every time one landed near Mary.

At last they arrived, and everyone piled off the coach into the warm sunshine. Roger Daley and Susan Rutt took charge by splitting everyone into two groups, with Daley leading the boys and Rutt taking control of the girls.

Daley marched off toward the rhinoceros enclosure with the boys straggling behind, leaving a flustered Rutt in his wake.

Stuart checked his watch. Just after 10 o'clock. They would have four hours in the wildlife park. This should be a fun escape from the tedium of his classes, but Stuart couldn't help his repeated backward glances towards the girls. There was only one he was interested in, and he couldn't make it too obvious.

The rhinoceros pen turned out to be a great distraction. A calf bounced around the enclosure with tireless energy, repeatedly charging and bouncing off his mother, who showed both annoyance and frustration.

'Look at him,' Harry pointed, 'he looks like you.'

'Could be worse. You look like the mother,' Stuart responded before ducking behind Paul. It was a wise move. If Paul hadn't been standing in the way, Harry would have launched.

'All right, you two. You both look like bloody rhinos, all grey and ugly. Let's head over that way to see the lions. Now that's my kind of animal.'

Even though Paul had calmed the situation, Stuart could feel Harry's eyes burning across the space between them. Stuart was sure his so-called friend would want payback, but for now, the distraction of the lions loomed. Five minutes later, Paul was shouting and thumping the reinforced glass which separated them from the wild beasts. A male lion lazed on a high wooden platform, its only action to emit an enormous yawn. The pounding on the viewing panel stopped as Paul spotted Daley heading their way.

'Sorry, sir,' he mumbled whilst turning away. As the trio moved into the shadows, Stuart cast a look about. The wildlife park covered a vast area and all the pupils seemed to have dispersed widely, despite their teachers' instructions to stay in one group. For two more hours, the trio wandered about aimlessly, crisscrossing over paths they'd already visited. They had two visits to the house where the fruit bats lived and three to see the reptiles, before finding themselves at the penguin enclosure.

Stuart looked on at the birds as they waddled about before diving into the water, where they would transform into majestic swimming creatures. Once submerged, they literally flew through the pool.

The image resonated. Throughout the day, he was a penguin, as he shuffled awkwardly behind Paul and Harry, looking for his place. Then, once he stepped away, a new clarity found him. He had time alone to think of Mary. Those thoughts had started out uncertainly, but soon a newfound excitement blossomed. Now she was on his mind every day, graceful, gliding thoughts.

For the second time that day, a painful dig in the ribs interrupted Stuart's concentration. He turned to see Harry sneering just inches from his face. 'If you ever call me a fucking rhino again, I'll make sure you feel like one has trampled you,' he threatened.

Paul stood across at the opposite side of the pool, so the menace went unnoticed. Stuart could feel his cheeks reddening as he rubbed his sore kidneys. Physically, he was no match to Harry, and the very idea of a punch up sent fearful tremors along his spine. He wasn't about to apologise, though. To Stuart, Harry clearly resembled a rhinoceros, well at the back end of one at least. He tried to ignore the bully and moved to the relative safety of Paul. The pain in his side would remain. Once Stuart sidled up, he could see his friend bore a frustrated expression.

'What's up?' he asked.

His friend ignored him, choosing instead to toss an apple in the air, which he skilfully caught. Stuart watched Paul's movement carefully. Something was clearly on his friend's mind. After he'd thrown the apple a few more times, Stuart winced as Paul simulated a throw which would have planted the apple smack into his face. He moved back a few paces. He didn't want to offer Harry another opportunity for violence. The backward step finally brought a reaction from Paul, who grinned mischievously.

There was only a small amount of threat, but Stuart had clearly seen it. Not for the first time, he considered his place. Who were his friends if he walked away from Paul and Harry? He knew he'd lost the trust of his classmates, and the very idea of having to take the school bus each day with Paul as his enemy gave him chills. He'd have to stick with it. He'd grown up with Paul and his friend wasn't that bad, really. Better to have his protection than to have him as an enemy.

The uncertain moment vaporised as Harry returned to the group, pretending that the dig in the ribs hadn't happened. 'Which one are you going to hit then?' he asked.

Paul spun around; clearly amused. Paul adopted the stance of a javelin thrower and pretended to throw the apple at the penguins whilst letting rip with absurd sounds as he pretended to obliterate the poor animals. There were too many people about for him to carry out the action. Stuart knew Paul would have happily bombarded the creatures for real if the opportunity had presented. The notion disgusted him but all he did was grin and join in with Paul's game.

Half an hour later, it was time for lunch. Although the park had designated picnic areas, there were also plenty of solitary benches around, and the three settled on one, which distanced them from the larger school group. They tucked into their food with gusto. As expected, Harry had a family sized bag of crisps, which he refused to share, though Paul grabbed a few. Stuart looked at his own pathetic bag and decided he wouldn't ask. Instead, he bit down on a salami sandwich, cursing inwardly as he'd told his mother he didn't like the filling. The day was warm, though, and his hunger won out. Stuart stared through the trees at the group in the distance and wondered what it would be like to re-join the main herd. Mary was there. That would be a big incentive. As before, he found himself distracted.

'Hey, Pratt. Come here,' Paul shouted.

Liam Pratt lived in the village and, like Mary and Paul, he would sit on the school bus each day, alone. Stuart felt uneasy as Liam looked up, a worried expression on his face.

Paul barked the order again and Liam shuffled across, head bowed.

'Aren't you eating?' Paul asked.

Liam held up his empty palms to confirm the obvious. Either he had no lunch, or he'd lost it somehow.

'Grab a seat. We've got extra you can eat.'

Stuart twitched. He saw the surprise on Harry's face. Liam edged forward, stopping several feet short.

Stuart looked on as Paul took out a paper bag from his rucksack, which he then opened. Inside lay four sugar coated doughnuts which Paul offered around. Despite having a mouthful of crisps, Harry took one and shoved it greedily into his mouth. Stuart waited. The treat with all its sugar coating looked enticing, but something felt wrong.

Liam must have sensed it too, but with Paul, Harry and Stuart all holding doughnuts and one left in the bag, he finally relented and took the last one. Paul smiled and took a bite, and Stuart followed suit. Warm chocolate oozed out from the centre, and Stuart's tongue embraced the treat. It was delicious. He closed his eyes to savour the cake, so missed the first sound of spluttering, but then Liam's sound became too great to ignore.

Stuart's eyes snapped wide. Whatever he was eating, poor Liam certainly hadn't received a chocolate doughnut. Paul and Harry were standing now, looming over Liam and blocking him off from the teachers and other students as the smaller boy choked and wretched.

'You're going to eat every mouthful of that, Liam, and we're going to make sure you do,' Paul grunted in a vile instruction.

Liam looked up, eyes pleading, and Stuart felt his face redden. He was part of the ring, preventing Liam's escape, and he watched on in horror as Liam took another bite. He could see the offending doughnut clearly now, and shame gripped Stuart until he, too, wanted to gag. He was sure a large piece of crusty dog shit lay inside. Stuart looked away. He wanted no part in this, yet his feet seemed to be glued to the grass. He desperately looked about, hoping for support, when he spied Roger Daley striding across the grass. A fresh fear gripped Stuart. He didn't want to be caught up in this horrible act. His eyes must have betrayed him as Paul looked up and saw the form tutor heading their way. All Stuart could do was watch as Paul reached down to grab the remaining half a doughnut and mash it into Liam's mouth. Both hands held Liam's mouth closed and, by pinching the boy's nose, Liam had no choice but to swallow. All the while, Harry grinned in delight and blocked the view of the approaching Daley.

Stuart felt sick. He wasn't sure whether his face was white or red, but what he'd just witnessed had crossed yet another line. He stared in disbelief at Liam's spluttering form.

'What's going on?' Daley asked when he finally arrived.

Stuart had no answer, but Paul spoke up as though everything was normal. 'Something seems to be stuck in Pratt's throat and he had a coughing fit, sir.'

Daley looked on, doubt on his face. He turned to Liam Pratt, who lay on the ground, crying. The entire doughnut had disappeared, and with it, any evidence of wrongdoing.

'Get up, Pratt, and stop being a baby. You're not choking, now get back to the class,' Daley said forcefully.

Liam rolled onto all fours before slowly standing and turning away. His posture showed defeat.

Stuart felt an inner pain. It felt much worse than the dig in the ribs he'd received earlier. He'd let this happen.

Upon Daley's instruction, they packed up their things and headed to join their classmates in the larger group.

For the rest of the day, Stuart seemed to be in a trance. Paul and Harry were laughing, but Stuart had no stomach for their actions. He merely nodded in the right places with no enthusiasm. He wanted to go home. He wanted to forget today had ever happened. Nothing could make him feel worse than he did now.

He was wrong. When the day finally ended, and Stuart exited the school bus in Ascot Midden, he saw Mary. As the coach moved away, she stormed up to him in a manner Stuart had never seen. Her normally pale face flushed, and he was sure she'd been crying. Spittle flew from her wide mouth as she spoke.

'I heard what you did to poor Liam. Don't you ever speak to me again!' she spat before marching off up the hill.

Mary's curt outburst stung. Stuart deserved her vitriol, and his mind turned inward to disgust. Liam hadn't even been on the school bus back to the village, further fuelling Stuart's sullen mood. A hard slap across his shoulder blades startled him from his gloom. It was Paul, grinning widely, as he had done all afternoon. He'd clearly heard Mary's outburst.

Chapter Seven

July 1982

SINCE THE TRIP TO the wildlife park, Mary had resolutely kept true to her word. At first, Stuart couldn't believe it, but as the weeks passed, she steadfastly refused to engage in any conversation. Worse, she actively moved away when he approached. A cartwheel of emotions spun throughout his brain every time he was alone. He'd started with shock before moving to self-loathing and finally came the anger. Some of this he directed inwardly, but over time those feelings faded and he recognised Paul and Harry for who they were.

He knew he'd broken a blossoming friendship with Mary, something he struggled to accept, but he also knew the awful bullying he'd allowed to happen to poor Liam. He, Stuart, had been part of it. He felt ashamed and sick every time he recalled that day. What made things worse was Liam's prolonged absence from the school. Stuart couldn't remember when he'd last seen the boy, certainly not for weeks. Nobody in the village had said anything, and the schoolteachers certainly weren't sharing. An empty desk and seat in the classroom, the only sad indicator of Liam's absence. Stuart wracked his brain, trying to remember who Liam had hung around with, but the kid had been a loner. So, with nauseating worry in his heart about what they'd done and no opportunity to make amends to Liam, Stuart set his brain on fixing things with Mary. The direct approaches had failed, so now, as the school holidays approached, he wondered about alternative strategies.

He reminded himself that separation from Paul and especially Harry would help. He was sure he'd detected a change in their behaviour as Paul nudged Stuart away from his inner circle. It felt odd. Stuart *wanted* out. He didn't want to be close to Paul anymore, and yet it would be on his terms only. He didn't want to be pushed out quietly like a piece of rubbish. No, Stuart couldn't go quietly. There would have to be a clear separation with him in control. The idea frightened him, but it was the only way he could see to rebuild Mary's trust in him. Mary *had* to see he'd changed, that he'd cast off the bad influences. He had to prove his reliability.

Whilst the school term ran, Stuart's idea seemed impossible. Harry and Paul loitered wherever he seemed to go and there was an ever-growing list of pupils who now distanced themselves. It wasn't just Liam and Mary who he needed to build bridges with.

As the bell sounded on the last lesson of the year, Stuart felt relief. At least this time, there was no mammoth assignment worth a few days of toil. Immediately Daley dismissed the class, allowing both Harry and Paul to shove their way out of the door. The pair sprinted along the corridor for the exit. Stuart hung back as the other pupils funnelled through the door at a calmer pace. He had over half an hour before the bus would arrive to carry him home and was in no hurry. The sun shone warmly, so even walking back to the village seemed an idea. Choosing this, Stuart set upon the walk home.

For the first time in months, he let his body relax. Normally he wasn't one for solitude; today, he embraced the moment. He swung right onto the track, which pointed to Nearwick, before a dog leg took him back to Ascot Midden. Dry ruts crisscrossed the path, slowing his progress. The terrain sent Stuart's mind back to childhood games where he had to navigate across a fantasy lava field. His erratic hopping soon ended when the track flattened out again, so he turned his attention to marvel at a kite which circled a few feet above his head. He found the picture captivating, and he envied the birds' freedom. Within the blink of an eye, the bird swooped down low, causing Stuart to peer through a hedge into the neighbouring field. There, nature enacted as Stuart knew it would. Some small rodent, its life extinguished in an instant. He shuddered at the brutal reality of what he'd witnessed. Why did everything always boil down to the choice of being predator or prey? Uncomfortable, Stuart's mind wrestled with both options as he struggled to find a better idea.

The walk home took almost an hour, and as the village hove into view, he could see the school bus disgorge a solitary passenger. He waited for the bus to pull away, and there she was, standing, no, glowing in the summer sunshine. He could feel his pulse quicken at the sight of her. Within the confines of school, there were always too many intrusions and starting would lead to derision. Here, today, Stuart was alone, standing in a shaded spot, and he could let his dreamy observation linger. As always, conflict radiated within. He wanted her to see him, but not yet. He had to prove his worth first. Today would be the start and with no sign of Paul, he felt sure of himself at last.

Mary didn't linger, though her pace remained slow as Stuart held back. He watched her progress in wonderment. It was clear as she climbed the hill where she was going. Stuart noticed how she dragged her feet with suggested reluctance. Soon she'd turned a corner, allowing him to follow unseen. Looking cautiously about,

Stuart set along the road. He couldn't see anyone about, though half the village could see this stretch of road and he wondered whether to divert across the fields. *Sod it*, he thought as he picked up the pace along the road. Seconds later, he turned the corner, expecting to see Mary in the distance. He felt disappointed when there was no sign of her.

Stuart slumped back into lethargy. Despite his despondent mood, he continued along the road, figuring a circular route which he could sell as an innocent stroll, should anyone ask. Nobody would ask, though. Nosy busybodies would natter and point, though not directly, and even his parents seemed absent from conversations these days. In an air of neurosis and muddle, Stuart walked on, unconsciously mirroring the dragging feet he'd seen from Mary earlier.

Soon he could see Mary's farm. Approaching undetected would be difficult, though not impossible, as Stuart climbed a gate which deposited him in an adjacent field. He didn't know who owned the land. It hardly mattered, he figured. An aged wooden post described a public footpath which he set along. The path would turn left away from the property before disappearing into a copse, but by then, Stuart would be close enough for a snoop.

He could see the cowshed now, though the hedge still blocked most of his view. Stuart had assumed there would be a break somewhere along the line, but so far, he was out of luck. He continued anyway, despite his uncertainty for being there. Ever since his departure from school earlier, Stuart felt as though some weird autopilot had engaged, and this was where he had to be.

He stopped, cocked his ear to one side, and listened. Everything was still, and he moved beyond the shed to a pair of barns. Here, his luck held as a small hope, offered a better view of the farmyard. Stuart crouched and watched. He could see the farmhouse properly now. The building looked an odd hybrid of impressive and neglected, structurally sound, yet dirty. He wondered whether the inside would look the same. He closed his eyes and imagined what it would be like to be across the threshold, only that he'd be in charge of the household. The lord of the manor image tickled him. He was as far away from a farmer as he thought possible, yet the idea appealed. Well, if Mary formed part of the picture, it held attraction, at least.

Seeing the earth was dry, Stuart lay down and wormed his way through the hedgerow and into the neighbouring field. He snagged his top but pushed through without further incident, though another damaged school shirt would need explaining. Fully aware he was trespassing, Stuart adopted a stooped shuffle to the edge of the barn. It wouldn't look good if anyone spotted him. This was the first time he'd seen Mary's home up close. Alongside the barn, Stuart sought a trough to crouch behind. Rust had eaten away to where the receptacle was nothing more than an eyesore, and the entire area stank. A nettle brushed his arm, causing Stuart to flinch. He cursed, but no one came and the yard remained deserted. The sting brought Stuart out of his dream.

Maybe being here wasn't a good idea. Why was he there? He knew, of course. Whether his actions were foolish, he couldn't decide, but this was all about understanding Mary and what better place to start? He grabbed a random leaf and rubbed his forearm. The plant certainly wasn't a dock, but he hoped the placebo would help.

From his vantage point, Stuart surveyed the area. He could clearly see two rows of four windows, though the angle of sunlight left them as dark pitted holes with no clues about what lay behind. Upstairs, curtains added another layer of mystery to the row of windows. Stuart studied the building as he considered where Mary could be.

He wasn't entirely sure she had come all the way home. But where else could she have gone?

Down the left of the farmhouse, Stuart observed a single door, which he took to lead into a kitchen. A pipe through which steam poured sat just to the side. Beyond that, he could see nothing. Deciding the yard ahead left him too exposed, he backtracked until he could circle behind one barn. There he found the going trickier with nettles and thistles conspiring to injure him. The drab grey school trousers kept the worst at bay, though it took a few minutes to cover the short distance. At last, he prised his body past a thick drainpipe to peer around the corner.

Stuart was no stranger to beautiful views of the Chilterns, but this view was spectacular. To the rear of the farmhouse, a long expanse of grass flooded the landscape, easing down to a river below. A narrow footbridge offered an escape before being swallowed by trees and a steep upward climb. It seemed obvious the land must be part of the farm, yet there was no activity.

Choosing to avoid plants which could injure, Stuart ducked down, returning to reconnaissance mode. The rear of the farmhouse was much closer; though the back mirrored the front and viewed from an angle there was no way he could see inside. He'd been right about the kitchen, though. That was one room he definitely could identify. He added the information to his mental map. The image was sorely incomplete as he wondered where Mary's bedroom lay. The mere thought seemed creepy, but he quickly brushed aside all feelings of inappropriate behaviour.

He felt stuck. He'd need to cross open space to see inside and in bright sunlight. He wasn't sure whether it would be worth the risk. Instead, Stuart returned to the practical task of safe information gathering. For starters, he wondered who else would be there. He had no idea, and this caused a trickle of fear running across his back. Nobody in the village ever spoke about Mary's family—not to him, at least. There had to be others, mother, father, siblings? *Where are they?*

Once again, Stuart was overcome with doubt. Although faded, the nettle sting remained, a gentle reminder he shouldn't be there. He found the lack of answers unsettling, though lacked the confidence to approach the farmhouse fully. The thoughts were distracting and Stuart leant away from the wall until he almost lost his balance. Only a quick grab of the drainpipe saving him. Suddenly, Stuart's eyes went wide as an upstairs curtain flickered. The shape of a person appeared behind.

He stumbled backwards, and this time went down hard. Any hope he'd fall upon soft ground evaporated as soon as he hit the floor. Sandstone rocks the size of his fist littered the area, sending jolts of pain across his lower back. Stuart groaned and rolled over slowly, stinging his palms against more nettles. He stopped moving and craned his neck, expecting to hear angry footfalls at any moment. *Have I been spotted?* No sounds came. He couldn't be sure if someone had seen him, though. No alarming shouts had sounded, but that could just be a ruse and even now somebody could charge towards his hiding place. His bravado wavered. Stuart reached out and gripped the drainpipe in readiness to haul himself back up. As he stood, the pipe shook and creaked, but held firm. The last thing Stuart needed would be to bring that down with an enormous crash. As he looked down, he could see his shirt offered an assortment of stains as grass, sweat, and a little blood intermingled. The small, dark droplets made up Stuart's mind. He turned to retrace his steps. It was time to go.

Mary had heard a noise upstairs and, knowing Keith had gone to Oxford, she carefully climbed the steps. As expected, her dad lay out cold in the first bedroom. Snorts and grunts echoed across the room and Mary recoiled at the aroma of vomit which clawed out onto the landing. She knew she'd have to clear the mess up again, but for now her interest piqued at the other sound she could hear coming from next door.

Sharp rasping breathing come from the other side of the door and Mary tensed as she gripped the doorhandle. She wondered who she'd encounter today, though pushed through anyway. Before her, shrouded in white, stood a figure. The creature barely moved, though Mary detected a fine shimmer as a skeletal hand gripped the curtain.

Mary had seen this before, though what had spooked her mother remained a mystery. She edged forward until standing alongside the figure in order to look out across the farmyard. Her mum just stared forwards, her face a blank page, its story erased many years before.

'Alright mum, let's get you back into bed,' Mary said while gently leading the way. The ghostly figure followed and settled in silence, allowing Mary to return to the window. Her eyes panned across to the barn and then the cowshed in the distance. At first nothing, but then she saw someone in the distance scuttle down towards the hedge. Just as quickly, the figure disappeared.

Chapter Eight

ROGER DALEY SAT BACK and lit a cigarette. He smiled before blowing a cloud of smoke across his classroom. The year hadn't been that bad after all. Craig Simmons and Susan Rutt had stayed out of his hair, though they had exchanged words over the Pratt boy. Accusations of bullying came thick and fast, especially in the aftermath of the trip to the wildlife park, but with no evidence, the voices soon faltered.

The boy's parents had removed him from the school soon after. It suited Daley. He didn't want another weakling; as fodder for his protégé, he supposed they had their use. Strictly, the word protégé wasn't correct, though Paul Winters had proven fun as a pawn to toy with. Daley dragged back more smoke and closed his eyes. Images from the rugby field as muddy, sweaty boys headed for the changing room filled his head. The mental dalliance didn't last. Soon he'd step away from the school to return to the privacy of his apartment, where the fantasy could play back in full. A cough in the doorway broke Daley's dream.

'Come on, Daley, you know you can't smoke in the classroom. Take it outside, will you?'

The voice was Craig Simmons', the head of the year. Daley offered a cool appraisal to his colleague before opening a window and flicking the stub out into the playground below. After pulling the glass shut, he rounded to face Simmons head on.

'There you go, Craig, no harm done. I'll be off then, unless there's something else you wanted.'

Simmons flushed, before straightening his back and recovering. 'There is something, actually. The head has summoned us to a staff meeting before we leave this evening. He has an announcement, apparently. We're due in the main hall in ten minutes.'

Message delivered, Simmons looked about uncertainly before disappearing into the corridor.

'Prick,' Daley uttered once his colleague had gone. Looking at his wristwatch, he saw it was almost 5 p.m. Another cigarette appealed, but his curiosity won. He got up and left the classroom.

The main hall could accommodate over a thousand students. Today, the expanse looked almost empty, with only fifty members of staff present. Daley, visibly reluctant, walked across the herringbone wooden floor, his shoes echoing loudly with each step. Most of his colleagues turned away as he approached.

Norman Jacobs had been the headteacher at Chancery's for over thirty years, overseeing a plethora of changes which he could not have foreseen when he took the job in the early fifties. Overall, though, it was felt that he'd made his mark. It was Jacobs who had fought governors and parents alike to allow girls to attend the school. Many had seen him as a heretic, but after a lot of controversy, they approved the move and things settled once more. Up on the stage, he coughed to gather his team's attention. A hush fell.

'Thank you all for attending. As you know, I've held the reins for over a quarter of a century. A few of you have had the misfortune to be here as long as I have.'

A titter rippled out across the room as Jacobs continued.

'The world is a different place from when I first walked through our gates. Our entire planet is shrinking as far-flung places flash across the news become part of our daily lives. I'm sure all of you have witnessed the successful ending of the Falklands conflict.'

A few nodded.

'It is regarding change why I've called you together today.'

Jacobs paused, looking at his audience. Most of the teachers met his gaze. Some looked away.

'I embrace these worldly changes, and I want my friends and colleagues to be among the first to hear my news.'

All eyes turned to the head. Everyone was paying attention.

'I am retiring from my position as head. This will be my last week in the job, and with many of you heading off for your summer holidays, this may even be our final meeting together.'

His grey eyes matted together as he waited for a response. Slowly, a gentle tap of applause ushered forth, becoming stronger. Some only patted their hands together in a fake-clapping gesture.

Jacobs continued, 'Whilst I am sure some of you will be happy to see me leave, I hope some at least will miss my hand on the tiller. This news, of course, is only half of the reason I called you all together today. As one departs, another must step up as leader. I'm sure you will all be as delighted as me by introducing your new headteacher, Craig Simmons.'

Jacobs beamed as Craig Simmons climbed the steps to join him on the stage. More applause followed as the pair shook hands warmly. Before Simmons could break his grip, Jacobs hoisted their arms skyward, as though one of them had just won a boxing match. It took a moment for Simmons to embrace the moment. The applause reached a crescendo with a few whoops and cheers being thrown in.

One figure stood rooted to the spot. Hidden towards the back of the assembled staff, Roger Daley's world had suddenly turned upside down.

Later that evening, Daley crushed an empty pack of cigarettes and threw them at the window. After a dull thud, the rubbish fell harmlessly upon the floor of his flat, offering no respite from his anger. 'Damnation!' he shouted, knowing full well his neighbours could hear. Daley didn't care.

The news of Simmons' appointment had floored him. How could he have been so stupid that he didn't see this coming? Everyone at the school must have known and now they'd all be laughing at him.

His eyes, red and sore, sought a drink. He snatched up a bottle of navy rum and cursed again, as only half a bottle remained. It would have to do. Pouring a generous measure, he sat back and contemplated the news. By the time he'd consumed the last measure of rum, Daley's mood had mellowed. He'd even wondered whether he could turn the circumstance to his advantage. The more he'd drunk, the more his thoughts darkened like the rum until finally he smiled wickedly. Next term, things were about to change.

Chapter Nine

August 1982

It had been more than a week since Stuart's visit to Mary's farm. The time had dragged. While outside the village hummed with activity, Stuart remained hemmed inside his bedroom. Paul had visited once, though Stuart had feigned illness and sent him away. The deception left him feeling nauseous; he wondered if this would be a sign of things to come. He didn't want to see anyone. Only Mary. And there was no way he could see Mary or even talk to her while he stayed here, cooped up in his bedroom.

Today, I'm going out, he decided. He didn't have any plan, and he certainly didn't want to see Paul, but along with a warm summer breeze came a refreshing confidence.

As he ambled along, an idea popped, and he headed towards the village store. He hadn't had many dealings with the owner, Phil Riley, though the little he knew offered encouragement. As the shop hove into view, Stuart felt his mouth dry as he wondered what he wanted to say. He felt incapable of talking to Riley. Riley's part of our village community, he thought. *I'm not. I want to be.*

He picked up his pace. Before his bravado could evaporate, he stepped into the shop. A bell chimed to announce him, though he needed to wait. Mrs Taylor, the old spinster from the opposite side of the village, seemed to spew gossip, which Mr Riley parried politely. Stuart moved away from the door until the smell of fresh bread and pastries caught. He smiled and took in the aroma as he waited. Standing behind shelves of produce, out of sight, Stuart listened to the incessant drone spouting from Mrs Taylor's lips.

After checking his pockets, Stuart selected a cake and moved to the counter, where he hovered nervously. Several awkward seconds passed until Mr Riley gestured in a vain hope Mrs Taylor would pause. The action worked. The older woman cast an annoyed, beaky stare at Stuart. Seeing she no longer had the shopkeeper's undivided attention, she strode off with purpose. The door banged shut loudly as she left.

'Thank you, Master Lockwood. I think you rescued me there. Don't share this, but that woman could talk for England and none of it is worth listening to. Now, how may I help you?'

Momentarily dumbstruck, Stuart placed the cake on the counter until his memory reminded him of the purpose of his visit. 'I was wondering...' he started as Mr Riley dug out a napkin to accompany Stuart's sticky bun. The words stuck in his throat as anxiety set in. This wasn't him. He didn't talk to adults.

Through glazed eyes, Stuart could see the shopkeeper was talking, though all he could hear was static. 'Sorry,' he finally blurted.

'I was just saying thank you. It can be a little tricky sometimes, planting smiles when one or two of my customers are thoroughly frightful. Tell you what, why don't you have the cake on me? You look in need of a decent meal.'

'Thank you, Mr Riley. There was something else I wanted to ask you.'

'Hey there. None of this Mr Riley malarkey. To my friends I'm Phil. Now, what can I do for you?'

Stuart became more relaxed. A few seconds earlier he'd been ready to grab the cake and flee the shop, now Stuart felt more settled than even in his own home.

'I was wondering if you need any help around the shop?'

He looked on as Phil spread his palms and gestured at the three aisles within the store. Each row held varieties of produce, and Stuart marvelled at how orderly everything was. He also realised how small the shop was and potentially how few shoppers there could be. He lowered his eyes. Suddenly, he didn't want to be there. His idea seemed absurd.

'Hey, just because I haven't got work here in the shop, it doesn't mean we can't help each other. Why don't you tell me what you want the money for and then I'll see if I can help you?'

'I want to buy a bike, as I'm fed up with taking the bus to school every day. I've already asked mum and dad if I can do some jobs over the holidays, but I looked in the catalogue and there's no way I can save up in time for the start of school.'

He looked on earnestly. Stuart had made his pitch and now his stomach churned as he stood waiting.

'How much extra do you need?'

Stuart blinked a few times before responding. 'I think with the money I should get from home, I'll need another fifty pounds. Do you have any work for me then?'

Phil clasped his hands together while he considered the request. 'I tell you what I'll do for you, or rather you can do for me. There are people around here who'd appreciate a delivery service. Mrs Barclay for one. She's over eighty and although she can make it down here on her own, she can't manage the walk back, not with a bag of shopping at any rate. In her case, she'd appreciate if you stopped for a while for a cup of tea and a natter. Do you think you could do that?'

Chatting with pensioners hadn't occurred to him. Stuart nodded.

'I have one condition, though.'

There it was. Stuart's heart sank. He knew the offer would be too good to be true. 'What condition?' he asked sullenly.

'You buy the bike straight away. You can pay me back with your parent's half or if you prefer, you can work for me a little longer until you've paid the entire amount off. What do you say? A bike would be handy, and if you delivered to the neighbouring villages, you may be in line for a bonus.'

Stuart spluttered with appreciation. 'Wow, yes, please,' was all he could muster.

The two days until the weekend seemed to take ages. Stuart had phoned and reserved his new bike and now, after lots of pleading, his dad had relented to help with collection.

'How come you've suddenly got all this money, then?' he'd asked.

'I told you, Dad, I haven't. Mr Riley has said I can work the summer helping with deliveries. He knows a bike will help, so he's paid up front.'

'Well, if you'd waited, I'm sure me and your mother could have put something by for your birthday.'

'I know, and I appreciate your offer, just that's months away, and I wanted the option of ridding to school instead of taking the bus each day. It'll save you the cost of my pass, won't it?'

His father returned a wry smile. Stuart thought his parents had little. He wasn't sure, really. They never spoke about anything of importance to him and even family meals around the table were sombre affairs. He thought some more. What were Mary's parents like? There had been a parent evening around Easter, but though he'd seen many of his classmates, Mary and her family were a no show. Still, he would have his bike soon and with it came independence and the first steps to build a bond with her, he hoped.

At last, they arrived. The bicycle shop looked more like a shed, with a workshop at the far end where a grey-haired man stood working. Rubbing his hands down his overalls, he walked over to introduce himself.

'Are you the young lad who called then? I'm the owner. My name is Jasper Wheeler —appropriate, really.'

He had clearly made the joke a hundred times. Stuart and his dad chuckled politely. 'So this is the one you're after then?' he continued, gesturing to a silver racing bike which stood propped against the wall.

Stuart's eyes bulged. The bike looked far too tall. Wheeler adjusted the saddle, and Stuart climbed on. The tips of his toes touched the floor, just. It was perfect.

Mary rarely ventured outside the farmhouse this summer. Each morning, Keith appeared with a list of chores. Each day, she silently complied whilst dreaming of the term to begin again and offer some respite. Hearing midday snoring as she so often did, Mary paused and looked at a blister which had somehow appeared unnoticed. This was how things were. Blisters, sores and other aches and pains weren't there and then suddenly pock marks and blemishes were all she could think about. Those were the worst times. Her heart sank and all the head demons came to remind her just how undesirable she really was. Not just to her useless family, but also to everyone she knew. It was so unfair. They didn't know.

She moved along the landing beyond the room where Keith lay unconscious. She loathed him. If only... The thoughts never lasted, always tempered that the authorities would lock her up and nobody would care for her mother. All her life, she'd been without parents, well, proper parents. With a zombie for a mother, a drunk for a dad, and a brute of a brother, a carefree existence had passed Mary by.

Her time within Chancery's had been scary at first, though a year in and her eyes had opened. She'd witnessed cruelty. Something she understood and despised. The trigger had been when she'd seen how others reacted. Some kids, especially the younger ones, were frequently beaten and robbed of their snacks or money. Most behaved as she did. They buckled, they cried, and they withdrew. For some, it was even worse. Mary feared for Liam Pratt. She hadn't seen him in the last days of the school year and now that everyone had escaped for the holidays; she knew she wouldn't cross his path. She wondered if he ever would return.

What had changed Mary's mindset was that, for the first time in her life, she'd stood up against bullies. At the wildlife park she'd confronted the boys, no, thugs. She did not know where her voice came from when she spoke out.

With the sound of Keith snorting nearby, Mary considered whether she could muster up the courage to stand up against her brother. Perhaps not yet, though she knew she couldn't sustain a lifetime of his abuse. For now, she had to consider her mother. Nobody else would.

She saw her mother, once again, staring through the faded curtains and out towards the hills beyond. Mary reached an arm around her and pulled her unresponsive parent into a hug. Together they took in the view, though only Mary was able to see the landscape. As always, something seemed to keep normality locked away and out of reach of her mother's senses. A hug would have to do.

Daley drew his Saab 900 to a halt within a gravelled bay in the Ascot Midden Nature Reserve car park. Ahead lay rolling countryside and a spectacular view across the valley below. A tatty wooden sign signalled the car park would be closed after 8 p.m. His wristwatch showed 4 p.m., plenty of time.

Only one other car occupied a space, its owners apparently rambling out of sight along one of the one of the hillside trails. That suited him. He didn't want anyone else around. A few seconds later, wearing a camouflage jacket, he strode north along a ridge before plunging down the hillside. In his arms, he carried a tatty old blanket along with a small backpack. Wooden steps helped his descent until a second path swept across. The sidelong path followed a tree line and, as planned, he cut right. The shade helped, though pockets of sweat still formed across his back and arms as he moved through the increasingly dense thicket. He had the option to remove his jacket, but declined as he blended in. Finally, the path disappeared in favour of a steep field heading down to the village below. Daley's eyes swept the area. Once he was sure there were no watchers, he picked up his pace to scurry across the gap. Ahead, a larger bank of trees loomed to swallow him up and beyond lay the sculpture trail. Although a public trail increased the possibility of witnesses, he was confident there would be plenty of places where he could stay unseen. Walking so close to tea time seemed to help with his seclusion.

Daley moved on through the woods. Soon he could see a figure wearing a bright red jacket loitering ahead. Daley's steps slowed to little more than a silent, approaching creep. Once the gap had closed to only a few feet, the figure turned and smiled.

Before Daley spoke, he peered beyond Paul, relaxing at last. 'Take that bloody jacket off, will you? Do you want the world to know you're up here?'

'It's not my fault. It's the only one I've got,' Paul responded. He took it off, showing mud-covered jeans and a dark green t-shirt.

'Better,' Daley said. 'I'm glad you're here. I wasn't sure you'd make the trip.'

Paul shrugged noncommittally.

Daley rubbed the grey stubble on his chin and lead the way back down the path. He waited until they'd reached the furthest part of the woods, where he deemed interruption unlikely, before he spoke again. Laying the blanket down carefully, he motioned for Paul to sit. The boy looked uncertain. Daley barked the instruction out.

Paul complied.

Daley reached into the rucksack and extracted two packets of crisps and a couple of different tinned drinks. 'Help yourself.'

Paul grabbed the ready salted along with a lemonade and then settled himself more comfortably. Seconds later the boy was crunching noisily, the packet half empty. Daley smiled, thinking of the year just gone and of what was to come. He waited patiently until Paul had devoured the snack, even chuckling when Paul let rip with a loud belch which echoed across the hill. He was sitting alongside now. The sweat returned as he considered what he was about to do.

He waited until he could clear the rubbish. 'Did you enjoy my class this year?'

The boy frowned. His shrug returned. 'I suppose so. It's school, isn't it?'

'True, though you've had it much easier than most. I'm giving you average grades when the work you turn in is full of shit. You must have noticed me allowing you to torment some of your classmates. I've even stepped in and diverted staff away so you could continue your bullying without getting caught. You owe me.'

Daley watched as the boy's cogs turned.

A nod.

Now came the risky bit. Daley felt confident he'd read the signs, but he could be wrong. He listened intently. Wildlife sounded everywhere, though no voices or footsteps echoed back to his ears. Now was the moment. Daley reached past the rucksack and placed his left palm on Paul's thigh. There was a brief flinch, and then both settled. Both knew. There had been no ambiguity in the movement. Daley was relieved to find out he'd been right. Those subtle lingering glances Paul had offered throughout the year may have been unintended. Paul may have even been unaware. Not now though. Now Daley could see confusion fall away into enlightenment in the boy's eyes. The sign Daley had been waiting for. Acceptance.

All Paul's bravado had gone. Here, alone in his bedroom where he could contemplate the world, he found his walls had come down. It was a weird feeling. Somehow he'd always known he was different. Now, instead of suppressing those feelings, he embraced them. It had taken Daley acting as a catalyst to push things forward. Paul lay back in the darkness of his bedroom, reliving the encounter over and over.

Together, the pair had opened a door and stepped through. There could be no going back. A new landscape lay before him, thrilling and disturbing in equal measure. Hidden away from prying eyes, he'd barely spent any time outside. His mother had fussed over the teatime absenteeism; Paul feigned a cold to stay upstairs as much as he could. He wasn't ready for their fussing, up close and in his face. Just the thought that his parents could prise open his innermost secrets with barely a glance frightened him and he wasn't used to feeling scared. Like a superhero, or even villain, he would need to lead two lives. It was the only way. Nobody could know what had happened up on the hill, or how it had made him feel.

There would only be one person he could confide in, and that was Roger Daley. Even thinking his name caused a confused and excited shudder. Finally, he dragged himself out of bed, dressed in scruffy jeans and a t-shirt and headed out. As he walked along the old rutted lane towards the hill, Paul could feel his body shaking in anticipation. Snapping a glance at his watch, he realised he was going to be late. Now, he felt a fresh fear. What if he missed his chance and Daley had already gone? That was *if* he'd turn up. Paul's breath heaved as he hastened up the slope. He had to be there. Paul didn't understand everything, but he couldn't let that one encounter be the only time.

Chapter Ten

Craig Simmons basked in his new status. The appointment had come as a surprise. There were formalities and procedures, of course, which went with any appointment of such prominence, but someone had swept the red tape aside.

Despite his best night's sleep in years, he yawned as he nudged past Ollie, his beloved spaniel, in order to collect the pile of letters which had just popped through the letterbox. Three brown envelopes sat ominously along an assortment of leaflets that would soon find their way into the bin. Brown letters always meant money. He scowled, though the top one held good news, at least. Simmons walked back to the kitchen, his insides radiating a warm glow as he read the contract. The verbal contract and assurances now backed up in writing formed a concrete bond. He really was the new head teacher at Chancery School.

Feeling a little smug, he rattled around until he found his expensive brand of coffee, which he scooped into a filter and set to percolate. He wouldn't be having instant today. Next, he placed four slices of bread into the toaster and set them to brown. Molly was still asleep, though Simons was sure his wife would appreciate him bringing breakfast through to her, especially with him waving the papers. She meant the world to him and already Simmons' brain sped up with ideas on how to spend the additional income.

Before the toast could pop, Simmons heard the letterbox rattle again. Assuming the postman had just returned with a forgotten letter, he paid no heed. *I'll scoop whatever it is when I take the coffee and toast upstairs*, he mused.

By the time the coffee was ready, Simmons' tray held a large plate of heavily buttered toast coated with a top layer of lime marmalade. Carefully he carried everything through to the hall, where he nudged the phone to one side before balancing everything upon the table. A solitary unmarked envelope lay there, white this time. Simmons scooped it up with confused eyes. He tore through the seal to examine the contents. Immediately, his hand shot to his mouth in horror. He lurched backwards, sending the breakfast clattering loudly across the carpet. A dark pool of coffee and grounds seeped into the patterned Axminster.

He dropped to his knees, one hand clasped across his mouth. The other hand shook uncontrollably until the paper fell to the floor. The contents were brief and made of letters cut from other papers or magazines. The message was simple.

We know your secret

Simmons' whole body sagged as a dozen questions bombarded his brain. *Who knew? What did they know? They couldn't know that, could they?*

He struggled to his feet before lurching to the front door. Shaky, sweaty hands pawed at the security chain, which refused to unclasp. Finally, he wrenched the front door open and peered out. In the distance, a dark figure vanished around the corner. 'Damn,' he shouted. Simmons knew the glimpse was fleeting and even now he questioned whether the person in the distance could have been male or female.

Mary had woken early. An hour or two of peace and seclusion presented. Keith wouldn't be up yet. She dressed and quietly patted along the landing, careful to avoid the spots where the floor would creak. Once downstairs, she headed out into the yard. The air felt cool, though this wouldn't last. Across the fields, mist formed beautiful wispy pillows that would melt away as soon as the sun rose higher. Spinning around, she turned her attention towards the village a little way off down the hill. As her head rotated, she recalled the figure she'd seen earlier in the summer. She was sure it had been a boy. Mary looked about again. She didn't fear the return of the intruder. Her concern lay with what her brother would do should they come back. Still, Keith lay asleep upstairs, so for now she could look around freely. She followed the outer perimeter of the outhouses until she saw a small gap in the hedge. Stepping forward, she knelt to inspect the hole. Smaller animals like a fox would have no difficulty in passing through and even she with her slim build could manage. Deciding she had plenty of time before Keith would appear, she wiggled through. Before her lay a path she hadn't trodden in years.

Memories of a time long passed flooded in, causing her to choke back a sob. She understood now why her father drank himself into oblivion each day. She figured having an automaton for a wife and no control over her condition must leave him feeling helpless. But it was tough for her too, as her mother was unable to connect with her daughter. There'd been glimmers when Mary thought she detected recognition, but just as quickly, the light in her mother's eyes petered out.

The sullen mood persisted as she continued down the hill. It was unlikely the intruder will have come from the opposite direction as the upward path appeared neglected and overgrown. No, this is where they'd approached from. At the end of the field, she mounted a stile and walked towards the village. Everything was still and at peace. This was her to a tee. She didn't enjoy encountering other people. Solitude is what she preferred.

A hush rested over the village as she came closer. Even the chirping crickets in the hedgerow had fallen silent. Mary whirled her body in an elegant dance, allowing her arms to lift and point skyward. Before she could complete a full arabesque stance, a bell tinkled, breaking her daydream. Her eyes squinted across the misty green. It was only Mr Riley, opening the shop to bring in the early newspapers. He waved at her and offered a wide grin. Mary shrank back, embarrassed at her display. The wave persisted as the shopkeeper beckoned her over. Mary considered the welcome. The man smiled and offered no threat, so she edged closer, wetting her ankles in the morning dew.

'Hi Mary. You're out early this morning. How is everything up at the farm?'

She hesitated, but responded, 'We're ok, thank you Mr Riley. How are you? Can I help you bring the papers in?'

'I'm glad to hear you're all fit and well. How could I resist such an offer? Here, if you could manage the smaller bundle, I'll take the rest. Just push the door open and pop them on the counter.'

Mary complied and carried the bundle through. Inside, the shop looked a little different. Some of this was the morning newspaper clutter, but across at one end lay neatly packaged parcels of groceries. That side at least looked to be very efficient.

'Thank you,' Riley wheezed as he bumped into the side of the door, causing the bell to tinkle again. Huffing, he deposited the papers, dug out a penknife and set about removing the string which held the pile together. Mary looked on with interest.

'Phew, these papers seem to get heavier every day. I'm lucky you were about. Maybe I should offer you a job like young Stuart.'

Mary's head flipped right to check she'd heard right. A school bully working in the local shop? Mr Riley seemed too nice to make such a poor judgement. 'He works for you? What does he do?' she asked, while trying to keep all traces of stammer from her voice.

Riley pointed at the neat grocery bundles. 'He's my delivery lad. I took a chance on him, and I'm really glad I did. Customers seem to like him and he's even done some favours for me.' Riley winked conspiratorially before continuing. 'We should really call Mrs Taylor, Mrs Trout. She's an awful gossip, but now Stuart does his deliveries, I barely have a visit. I used to have an awful job getting her out of the shop. The dreadful woman wouldn't take a hint.'

Mary smirked. The rant came as a refreshing change from a man whom she considered as friendly and kind.

'And, there's Mrs Barclay. Don't tell Stuart I've told you this, but he stops around at hers for a cup of tea with biscuits. The old dear loves his company.'

Mary smiled politely. 'I won't tell,' she said, almost in a whisper. 'I'll leave you too it, but if I'm about early again, I'll help you bring the papers in.'

With that, she headed for the door. Once outside, the mist had thinned, but her skip returned. Mr Riley's comments came as a revelation. Maybe Stuart wasn't so bad after all.

Chapter Eleven

September 1982

THE CLASS ASSEMBLED NOISILY in the great hall. This year things seemed to be organised and certainly drier. Stuart looked on as other senior year students joined the gathering. He looked along the line of classmates, all chattering excitedly, though none spoke with him. At the opposite end, his eyes settled upon Paul, who turned and offered a sneer before looking away.

Stuart paused in consideration. He'd suspected this would be Paul's response to being ignored across the summer. Mentally, Stuart had spent weeks preparing to resume his time at school. He was sure his action to step away would land him in trouble, and now, as he caught a malevolent stare from Harry, he knew things would get rough. Ahead in the next row stood Mary. She seemed to be unaware of any adolescent hostility which bubbled behind her. The noise levels dropped. Looking about, Stuart detected Mr Simmons taking to the stage. This year he looked different. This year he wore a long flowing gown which draped gracefully across his shoulders and down almost to the floor.

Stuart listened along with the others, though it was only after a few minutes had passed, when they could finally take their seats, that he realised Simmons had assumed the role of headteacher. The change came as a surprise and, like most in the room, he wondered how this would affect him personally. So far, his perception of Simmons wasn't good, but then he couldn't cast any bad thoughts, not when his opinion of himself hovered around the gutter.

The speech finally ended and the teaching staff looked ready to disperse. Daley and Miss Rutt were up there, as well as other new staff. Even his own year group had fresh faces. Stuart had warmed to Hugo Perez, whom he'd affectionately christened Penfold on account of his tanned skin and endearing quality of saying 'crikey,' at the end of most sentences. Only the dark curly hair and glasses strayed away from the image of Danger Mouse's sidekick, though that was enough to catch the bullies' attention.

There were other newcomers. The nasty crowd had already renamed Jonny Mohungu to Jonny Monkey, and Linda Hooper's downfall came in the guise of a stutter. Jonny had the misfortune to live on the same estate as Harry, while Linda had moved into Ascot Midden over the summer. He had only met them briefly. Would he make friends with them? He knew he'd made a statement. Six weeks of school holidays had passed and during that time Stuart had only seen Paul once; that encounter had been an accident. He cringed when he recalled a trip to the local baths. The swim had been fun, and he'd enjoyed the floats and other floating debris the leisure centre offered. He'd even seen a few semi friendly faces, that was until he saw Paul and Harry's ominous presence.

When Stuart finally climbed out of the pool, he felt small and vulnerable. Both Paul and Harry stared at him through narrow eyes. He'd acknowledged them with a nod as his shaky legs carried him forward. He knew he'd renounced their friendship. The ongoing absence over the remaining holidays had only offered confirmation. Even the bike ride in place of the school bus had been an explicit statement and as Stuart looked along the line again, he could feel a tremor run across his lower back.

The assembly finally wound down, allowing Simmons to dismiss the pupils to their respective classes. The noise picked up as chairs scraped and children and teaching staff alike headed for the exits. Ned Fairclough, the head of science, approached but Simmons waved him away, while mopping away the sweat on his forehead. Half stumbling, he headed for the sanctuary of his office.

Once inside, he slumped against the door, using his shoulder to push it closed. Somehow he'd held everything together; now alone, he crumbled. It took an enormous effort to move across and pull the blind, but he couldn't risk anyone outside looking in. He collapsed in a padded leather chair. Even pouring himself a whisky seemed to be momentarily beyond him, and he had to rest the decanter down before the golden liquid could spill across his desk.

Finally he managed a generous measure and the burn which hit the back of his mouth eased his shaking. Within seconds, the double shot had vanished down his throat. The drink offered the medicine Simmons needed. Dabbing his forehead again, his mind returned to consider all the threats he faced as he'd done a hundred times before over the previous weeks.

During the assembly, he'd tried his best to scout out everyone in the room. Now, realisation hit him. There were too many students in his school and coupled with the staff and the possibility his tormentor may not even be there, his situation seemed hopeless. The only hope he had was that the threatening letter had been a one off. But how could it be? Someone wanted to bring him down and he had absolutely no idea who.

For Harry Blake, the holidays had been a glut of hard work. Not chores, those were for the worthless scum he looked down upon every day at school. No, the sweat and pain he'd endured were all self inflicted. His first years had been fun, that is, if you filtered out all the lessons. Academia would never be for him.

Harry planned to take what he wanted at every opportunity. Within his own year group, this proved to be simple. He was taller and stronger, so ripping lunchboxes off the weak was easy. There were older bullies in the school, of course. Harry watched them and learned their methods; they were bigger than him and more organised. He knew that he was a small fish in a big pond and that was something he set about changing over the holidays. Living miles away from Paul offered a bonus. It meant more time for himself during the summer. He'd always loved to watch the Saturday afternoon wrestling as Kent Walton welcomed the audience with the phrase "Greetings grapple fans", but now American wrestling had taken over with Jesse Ventura being his favourite. Even the third Rocky film with its catchy "Eye of the Tiger" theme fuelled his machismo.

Training didn't start well with aches and pains conspiring to taunt his brain. Yet he persisted. He didn't know what he was doing, so he watched the odd video to have an idea. Slowly his self enforced boot camp brought about noticeable results. Now Harry had the physical ability to back up his intimidating persona.

During the first assembly back, he'd sat with Paul as always. The pair had laughed despite being threatened by the teachers, though finally they'd quietened down. Harry yawned as the dull speech threatened to send him to sleep. Every so often Paul would grip his arm to stop him from toppling forwards. Harry didn't mind. He was certain every time Paul nudged him, his friend would feel a wall of bicep. The class that followed seemed equally dull. What was the point of history, anyway? Harry felt his eyelids droop once again as their teacher, Mr Knowles, drawled on about two people called Maud and Stephen. Maybe if Maud had been a looker like some women in old paintings, he'd have shown interest. Geography followed... boring, he thought. Eventually lunchtime came, and Harry mimicked a liquified body by sliding off his seat.

'Come on,' Paul teased, yanking hard on his elbow to pull him up and lead him towards the door.

Outside, a dozen classmates were chatting loudly; even Harry's looming presence didn't subdue them.

'What are you lot yacking about?'

The response was immediate. 'Haven't you heard? We've just had PE and Foster got an erection in the changing room.' A titter of laughter greeted the news.

Harry knew who Anthony Foster was and offered a look of contempt before turning to Paul. 'Come on, we're not having any bloody queers in our school.'

Paul was shocked and looked aghast. Realising he needed to hide his feelings, his face became a mask. He followed Harry as the pair headed down to the changing rooms.

The door creaked as they both pushed through before finally settling into silence. The atmosphere broke to the intermittent sound of someone blubbing. Paul wanted to hold back but Harry grabbed his wrist, insisting he follow. Ahead lay the changing room. Along two walls sat bench seating with pegs above, all empty. The sounds were louder now, echoing out from the communal shower area.

Harry's knuckles clicked loudly as Paul edged around the corner. Foster lay slumped on the floor. The boy's eyes seemed red, raw and harsh against the stark whiteness of the tiled floor, his body barely covered. He was shaking and mumbling, 'I didn't mean for this to happen,' over and over again.

Without warning, Harry stepped up and kicked hard, aiming for the boy's groin. He missed by inches, but Paul grimaced as though he could feel the pain. An inhuman howl echoed across the chamber, only punctuated by a second kick. This one landed properly and a new gurgling splutter was all Foster could manage in response. Paul's eyes went wide, and a lump formed in his throat as he watched the beating.

Then the worst thing happened. Harry stood back and pointed for Paul to do his part. 'Come on. What are you waiting for? We don't have any fucking poofs in this school.'

For the first time ever, Paul froze. Harry noticed it as he latched onto Paul's shoulder to shove him out of the way.

'Hey, leave off. I'm just lining him up for the best shot,' Paul responded angrily.

An inane grimace returned to Harry's face, and the bully stepped away. Paul gulped. Until then, hurting kids had come easily. Why was it so difficult this time? Paul stepped back two paces until he nudged the opposite wall. He blanked out, unable to think about his next action. He swept forward and his right foot connected with Foster. Hard. Another sickening howl erupted, followed by the noise of running footsteps.

'What the hell is happening here?' Daley shouted, louder than Paul had ever heard. The teacher's face flushed puce and flecks of saliva flew out. He repeated his question, more vehemently.

Paul flushed and couldn't speak. He looked vulnerable. Foster, on the floor, was writhing in agony. Harry, stepping up, broke the silence.

'We found him like this, sir.' His look one of defiance.

Whether Daley could see the blatant lie for what it was or not was unclear as Paul's mind leapt in frantic overload. He couldn't read his teacher's mood. All he saw was shaking, and that came from everyone in the room. Slowly, his senses returned, and he reached down in a weak attempt at help. Foster had his head buried, but Daley moved on to intercept before the pair got too close.

'Right, you two. Get up to the office and find the nurse. Send her down here right away.'

Both boys stepped back and edged toward the door. Harry full of bravado, Paul was timid. He couldn't understand why Daley would excuse them. He noticed Harry's step getting more confident. *Bastard*, Paul thought bitterly.

Before they could reach the corridor, Daley shouted after them. 'And make sure you both come and see me after school.'

'What the hell happened?' Simmons raged. 'He's been beaten black and blue and now I need to meet with the parents.'

Daley crossed his legs and reached for a cup of tea before responding. An act which further fuelled Simmon's fury. As Daley took a sip, Simmon's patience snapped, and he thumped a fist on his desk. The gesture achieved little apart from hurting his hand as Daley merely placed the cup down as delicately as if he were attending a garden party.

'I don't know, headteacher. There are several versions and as yet I haven't rooted out the truth from anyone. Clearly someone has beaten the Foster boy, but so far, I'm at a loss to identify the culprit.'

'What about Winters and Blake? I heard they were in the area and wouldn't put it past either of them to attack a child.'

'I'm sorry, headteacher, but I think you are barking up the wrong tree there. I walked in only seconds after them, so they couldn't possibly have had enough time to carry out the assault.'

'What about the boy? Has he said anything?'

'Too shaken up apparently, though I will, of course, supervise his questioning personally. You have my complete support for this matter. I, for one, will not tolerate violence in our school.'

'What kind of violence do you advocate, Mr Daley?' Simmons asked in an unusually perceptive jibe.

Daley cleared his throat. 'What I mean is there will always be violence within society, but we have an army and police to deal with such things. It's their job to keep everything civilised.'

Simmons let his gaze linger as he tried to find out what had happened and what part Daley had played. It wouldn't come. He briefly toyed with the idea that Daley could have delivered the threat a few days earlier, before remembering he'd glimpsed a boy running off. It chilled him to think of the note, though there had been no more threats and, as yet, no revelations. Suppressing his fears, Simmons tried to convince himself the act had merely been a sick prank. Quickly, he flipped his attention back to Daley. It was unclear whether his junior colleague had detected Simmons' lapse, but he had more pressing problems today. Inwardly shaken, Simmons dismissed Daley with instructions to be updated later on that day. Once alone, he reached for the decanter.

Paul looked forlornly at the classroom door when the bell sounded to signify the end of school for the day. Glancing at his watch, he saw he had twenty minutes before the school bus would depart, leaving him stranded. As the pupils funnelled out into the corridor, he waited along with Harry. Both had spent the day in contemplation, and Paul was dreading the meeting with Daley. Everything had been quiet since the incident, well, from the teaching staff at least. His classmates were a different story. Animated conversations where words like "hospitalisation, police and gay' seemed to be bandied about, caught his ears every time. He knew their behaviour had crossed a line and there would be consequences. Harry didn't seem to mind as his mate blatantly suggested Foster had it coming and the boy was too much of a coward to blab. Paul couldn't be sure and found Daley's rage earlier unsettling.

The room finally emptied and fell into a moody hum comprising the gentle chatter of hundreds of escaping children. The realisation that everyone was fleeing, except for them, hit Paul hard. He felt sure he could feel his breath rasping as his heart rate inched upward. Realising this, he moved away to the window. Paul didn't want Harry to see him like this. Before his mood could sour any further, the door sounded and Daley walked in. Both Paul and Harry appeared startled before meekly sitting on adjacent desks where Daley had signalled. Their tutor closed the door firmly before dragging a chair to the front of the class, which he spun around, allowing him to sit with legs splayed and forearms resting across the top.

'Well. You two sure fucked things up.'

With their classmates absent, the room took on a new darker feel, rooting both boys silently to their seats.

'Sir,' was all Paul could manage.

'So, where shall we lay the blame if we're going to get you out of this mess?'

'Sir?' Paul repeated in confusion.

'Well, I've given you a lifeline by saying I got in there just after you did and when I spoke with Foster earlier, everything that came out of his mouth was pure garbage. You certainly did a number on him, that's for sure. He won't be pointing the finger soon. But, if he does, we'd best get another patsy lined up to take the fall. Who's it going to be?'

Paul digested Daley's comments before looking to Harry for support. Neither knew what to say. Daley continued.

'What about Stuart Lockwood?'

Paul, taken aback, considered the suggestion. Daley's idea seemed absurd, though the more he thought about it, the more the idea stuck. Stuart would have it coming after he'd abandoned their friendship. Looking across, he saw Harry's wide, beaming smile.

'Good, that's settled. I'll nudge Foster into making an accusation and in the meantime, you two had best lie low. Now, get out of here.'

Just as Paul and Harry reached the door, Daley made one last comment. 'Don't forget who saved your arses. You both owe me and don't you forget it.'

Chapter Twelve

MARY LOOKED OUT AT the fields as the school bus pulled away. This was her favourite time of day. From her prime vantage point, she could see the beautiful countryside and today blue skies sat perfectly above the green grass and trees. Even the recently harvested fields offered a wonderful glow, and above the thriving population of kites swirled elegantly to complete the picture. She sighed in a rare display of contentment. That morning she'd only seen her mother, though she needed to creep quietly when she left the farm. The others remained asleep, allowing her a peaceful walk down to the bus stop. Even the sight of Paul hadn't burst her bubble. True, she couldn't trust him. He appeared to be like her brother only in a different guise, but today he kept away, skulking silently at the rear of the coach.

As the vehicle approached the top turn out of the village, she saw Stuart peddling gently towards the school. He, too, appeared happy. She hoped he was, and the notion stirred her own emotions. Once beyond the turn, the road widened and the bus could overtake, leaving Stuart in their wake. The bus ride would take another fifteen minutes, which Mary used to continue her happy daydream. This morning, Stuart featured heavily as she delved into fantasy where they were together, somewhere safe. Somewhere her mother was safe, somewhere the others couldn't harm them. She knew her dream was unrealistic, especially since she'd barely spoken to Stuart in months, but today could just be the day where her chance to breathe life into their relationship would come.

Stuart locked his bike in the rack before heading to his first class of the day. It was only the second day of term and, being late summer, he'd experienced a lovely ride in along the warm country lanes. He'd even seen Mary look down at him when the bus came past, causing him to peddle a little harder in a futile attempt at keeping up.

The first lesson would be biology. Not his favourite, though all the other classes for today suited him. Best of all, he shouldn't have to get too near to Harry or Paul, as Daley didn't figure in that day's timetable. The usual cluster of pupils milled about listlessly, waiting for the summons of the bell. He waved at Perez, who grinned and waved back, showing Stuart he hadn't burnt every bridge. Just as Stuart ambled over, he caught Daley in his peripheral vision. He slowed, hoping to go unnoticed, but it was no good. The teacher waved him over.

'Lockwood. You need to come with me immediately.'

Stuart's heart sank. No good could come of this. He meekly followed, keeping several paces behind. Once inside, Stuart knew where they were heading and, sure enough, Daley knocked on the head's door a moment later.

'Come.'

'Thank you, headteacher. I've brought with me the culprit.'

Stuart froze. Surely, he couldn't have heard right. *Culprit, for what?* Simmons' face twisted into a sneer, causing Stuart's heart rate to spike. The door closed behind, trapping him. A sofa sat along the edge of one wall along with two wooden backed chairs. No one offered a seat.

'What have you got to say for yourself then, Lockwood?'

Stuart's face showed a mosaic of confusion. 'I'm sorry sir, can I please ask why I'm here?'

Without any warning, Daley slapped Stuart below the ear. 'Don't be impudent, boy. We all know why you are here. There were witnesses, you know.'

This revelation stung. *Witnesses? To what?* And then he realised. Surely they didn't think he'd attacked that boy? The lurch within the pit of his stomach told him they did. 'I... but sir, I don't know who told you, but I have done nothing.'

Daley weighed in. 'Well, you'd better come clean. That Foster boy identified you. I believe the child's parents will be in later on today and they will expect the school to take stern action.'

The walls closed in on Stuart as Daley continued. This was impossible. Surely someone had seen him outside when the attack had happened. Stuart searched his brain for a glimmer of an answer that could save him. It seemed they'd decided his guilt before he'd even arrived. With Daley controlling proceedings, Stuart looked towards Simmons in the hope the head's authority would help quell the inquisition.

The head looked uncomfortable, though Stuart's pleading eyes seemed to force a shift.

'Mr Daley is indeed correct. Foster's parents will be here later on this morning. From what I gather, poor Anthony is in complete shock. I spoke with Mr Foster briefly yesterday afternoon and so far I've persuaded him to keep the police out of this, however we need to mete out a suitable punishment. I think is it best for everyone concerned if you just come clean right now.'

'But I have done nothing. Believe me.'

'Were you not listening, boy?' Daley roared. Simmons cringed. 'There were witnesses. You either own up now and save the entire school embarrassment, or we give you over to the police. What's it to be?'

Stuart crumbled. He knew they planned on throwing the book at him. It was the threat of police involvement which tipped the balance. He looked on in silence.

Simmons asserted himself. 'Well, Mr Daley, I think we can both agree the school would suffer badly if this gets out. Best, I think if we take action immediately.' The head turned to Stuart. 'Given there are witnesses and you are choosing to remain silent, I can only conclude your guilt. You had best get yourself off home.'

'Sir?' Stuart queried, feeling broken.

'I will, of course, be writing to your parents, but there will be no further need for you to attend this school. I am expelling you.'

Phil Riley had heard a rumour and, judging by how Stuart approached his shop, he considered there could be some strength to the stories. He wasn't about to let Mrs Taylor affect the judgement which had served him all his years and had, so far, been sound.

'How are you, Stuart? You look down in the dumps if you don't mind me saying.'

'I suppose you've heard what happened?'

Riley scratched his chin thoughtfully. 'I heard something, but I don't pay too much heed. Why don't you tell me your side and then I'll decide?'

Stuart leaned in until his elbows brushed the counter and then his head dipped into both hands. He sighed. 'I can't go to school anymore.'

'Can't or won't?'

'Can't. They've expelled me.'

Riley let out a long whistle. 'And what did your folks say about that?'

Stuart buried his head in his hands and let out a groan.

'It mortified mum. She keeps on about how I've let everyone down and how everyone in the village must talk about them. Them, for god's sake. It isn't them, it's me that this is all happening to.'

'What about your father? Did he take the same line?'

'Oh, god, no. He's worse. I told him I didn't do what they say, but he ignored me. He says the school must have their facts right, otherwise they wouldn't have booted me out. Sorry, Phil. I don't think I'm much good to you or anyone today.'

Stuart stood upright before Riley gestured for him to remain.

'Sounds like a heap of trouble and no support. The way I figure it, I still don't know what happened and damned me, I won't pass judgement on anyone until I'm sure of the facts. Now, you can head out of that door and I won't make any attempt to stop you, or you can spill your guts and I'll listen without giving you too hard a time.'

For the next fifteen minutes, Riley kept silent. When Stuart finished, he repeated his low whistle.

'They can't do that, can they?'

After Stuart's animated offload, the glum demeanour returned. 'Do it, they've done it. I'm gone. No way I can go back to Chancery's.'

'But from what you've told me, you didn't attack the kid. If you say you didn't, then that's good enough for me. There is one thing which worries me, though. Why did a teacher and some other witnesses say you did?'

'But you said you believe me.'

'Whoa. And I do. I just want to know why they would set you up like this. Do you know who said this stuff?'

Stuart considered the question. 'There was some talk that Paul from the village and his thug mate Harry made gay threats before storming down there and apparently Mr Daley had walked in on the attack, but he's a teacher and everyone believes the crap he tells them. Why won't they believe me, Phil?'

Riley patted him on the back and shook his head. 'I don't know, son. I don't know.'

Mary had heard the rumours from multiple sources and most seemed to follow a similar, disturbing story. Whispers flowed around the school, swirling like a layer of mist. With each comment added, the venom increased until the mist had turned into an impenetrable fog. She didn't believe the stories, though one thing seemed obvious. Stuart had left the school.

Stuart had a few allies who remained. Perez, Mohungu, and Hooper all remained loyal, but without Stuart to give his side of the story, their voices quickly drowned out. There were other rumours, though. These were quieter, as though those spreading the tales feared Daley's reach. The whispers suggested something entirely different. Those stories pointed directly at Paul and Harry. Having witnessed their behaviour first hand, Mary knew which story she believed, though without Anthony Foster around to corroborate, she'd struggle to find any truth. The entire episode had added another sour layer to how she saw life and people. Not for the first time, she wondered where all the good guys were.

Simmons looked at the wall clock and urged it onward to the end of the school day. The meeting with Foster's parents had been fractious, though they'd accepted the expulsion as a suitable punishment. It had been touch and go whether the police would become involved, but he'd calmed that storm. He was glad Daley hadn't been there to fan the flames. The meeting had lasted less than half an hour. To Simmons, the time had dragged. Anthony hadn't attended, which came as a surprise. It irked Simmons. Everything about the attack story seemed riddled with holes and without the boy telling him face to face, Simmons' mind remained full of doubts. Instead, he listened patiently to both parents about how dreadful everything was, while nodding sympathetically. In the end, he convinced them that the school had quickly dealt a harsh punishment.

Now he sat alone again, his thoughts returned to the pressures of the job. Already, only two days into the new term, he felt exhausted. Surely, his predecessor, had had things easier.

Chapter Thirteen

December 1982

PAUL HAD MET ROGER Daley secretly three times across the autumn term, each time in the same location. On the first of these, nothing physical happened, instead the pair just talked. It had been weird but it allowed Paul to gush his feelings. Daley's response was to listen. That meeting turned out to be just what Paul needed. It had been chaos in his head after the attack. Not just the vicious attack or Stuart taking the fall but Paul felt guilt-ridden. There was no way he could share his feelings with Harry, though his thug friend did at least accept Daley had saved their bacon. For a while Harry had toned things down, which helped. Paul could see that it was only temporary; he was sure Harry would soon be back to bullying again. The only sour note had been Daley's whinging about Simmons' appointment to head. Every time they were together, he drawled on, saying it should have been *him* running the school and how much he wanted to push Simmons off a cliff and step into his job.

Now Christmas approached, and Paul found his mood take a dip. Where others broke up in jubilation, Paul would head back to the village and self-imposed isolation. He didn't like winter. Yes, there were good things like the holiday food and the occasional snowball fight if the weather would ever deliver enough, but he despised the cold and wet. Even his other meetings with Daley had been a washout, just a few minutes of clumsy fumbling before both got too cold.

He climbed onto the school bus home for the last journey of the year. No ridiculous assignment this year; he smirked as he watched the first years shocked chatter. Mary was one of the last passengers to board. Paul studied her. He felt something stirring but was that possible for a gay man? He could see her body changing, and just for a fleeting moment, a confusing thought passed. How would it feel to get really close to her? How would it feel to share a kiss?

Simmons sat back and smiled widely. He'd safely negotiated his first full term as head and, apart from some wobbles in the beginning, he felt his management of the school had gone well.

Foster's parents had taken the boy away, deciding home schooling would be safer. It suited Simmons. He didn't want constant reminders every time he walked the corridors. Privately, he acknowledged two pupils had departed due to bullying within the calendar year. In a school his size, mistakes would always happen, he reasoned. Deciding he deserved a celebratory drink, he poured a generous measure. As with the failings which surrounded him, he also ignored his increasingly ruddy complexion.

A knock on the door.

'Yes?' he barked.

The school secretary entered, her eye immediately on the whisky glass. She looked disapprovingly.

'What is it?' he blustered, knowing she'd seen him drinking too often.

'Just bringing you the last items of post before we break up. Christmas cards mainly.'

Simmons snatched the pile and shooed her away. He couldn't be bothered with her anymore. She left promptly, allowing him to finish the glass in peace.

It looked like she'd been right. A dozen cards plopped onto his desk for him to peruse. Some envelopes sat invitingly in red, another in gold, but one stood out. Simmons' fingers shook as he inspected the paper wrapper. Feeling uneasy, he tore across the seal to reveal the contents. Just as before, a carefully crafted note dropped out. Again, the sender had cut letters from other publications to form a cruel mosaic message. Simmons' world spiralled downward once more.

Soon be time to tell

Chapter Fourteen

January 1983

DALEY CHUCKLED FOR THE umpteenth time that morning. Perched upon a chair at the front of the classroom, he rested both feet on his desk and sighed. He knew Simmons wouldn't have had a pleasant holiday, but then the idiot wasn't right for the post.

Sending threatening notes had been one of his better ideas and, with the slowdown for the holidays, delivering it unobserved had been easy. Stating "we" in the first message only added another layer of subterfuge. He hadn't decided whether he would follow through with the threat. For now, the mere act of shaking the head's foundations seemed to be enough. He'd seen Simmons earlier when he'd arrived. The winter certainly hadn't been kind. Daley looked on in amusement as he counted the signs of strain that appeared to weigh down upon his senior colleague. Drooping eyes, grey thinning hair, a face etched with weary lines, all were on show. Even Simmons' movement seemed to sag under a weight of worry. Hopefully, others would see the signs too, Daley grinned. If not, he'd act again.

While he waited for the class to arrive, bringing with them the joy of ridicule as he could tear into their feeble Christmas assignments, he let his thoughts hover over his relationship with Paul. Relationship was the wrong word. It was intimacy, mutual consent, despite what anybody would say. Still, he knew they would have to be careful. He toyed with the idea of Paul visiting his home before dismissing it. He'd done that once before, many years ago, and the outcome had been a disaster. No, he wouldn't make *that* mistake again. Could he afford to rent a second flat? He quickly dismissed that notion as too expensive. For that to work, he'd need a pay rise and to get that extra wage, he'd need to oust Simmons.

In his office, Simmons examined the second note, tucked away in the desk drawer. Ignoring the paper over the holidays had achieved nothing. On his journey in that morning, he'd tried in vain to pretend it had been a horrible dream.

He lifted the envelope and held the document, examining it for clues. There were none he could see; his own pawing had smudged any fingerprints. Even if he hadn't destroyed it, who could he ask to check? He'd wrestled with taking the letter to the police, but every time he thought about it, he rejected the idea. He didn't even have the first note anymore, had thrown it away that fateful day, afraid Molly would see it. It had gone. Now all he had was the second threat, which he held in his hands nervously. The temptation to shred it was great. He hovered over the shredder before deciding against it.

He returned to his desk, where he locked the note away, deciding he had a job to do.

Chapter Fifteen

April 1983

IT WAS EARLY MORNING and Mary busied herself with her usual morning jobs. Today, she could take her time. The Easter holidays meant no school. While others rejoiced and ate copious amounts of chocolate, Mary found only solitude. A snort sounded behind her and she spun, expecting to see Keith but it was her father. Her nose wrinkled in bilious disgust. His bloodshot eyes barely registered her presence. Before she could move away, the smell hit, forcing her hand to her mouth. Everything from his skeletal frame through to his lumbering gait suggested decay.

Mary turned her head in fright before falling back into the shadows. She hoped he hadn't spotted her so he would not hit her like before. She'd convinced herself the blow had meant nothing, her father was a victim of the booze, his behaviour not his fault. Her father moved off before attempting to spit out of the window. He missed, leaving a large gob of phlegm to meander down the pane. Seconds later, he'd returned to his bedroom and a dull thud echoed.

She waited, wanting to make absolutely certain he had collapsed before she ventured into the light. She didn't check up on her father, couldn't care less. The days when Mary tried to comfort and resuscitate had gone. Mary turned instead to look after her mother. Sitting astride her bed, Mary took out her favourite brush and set to work, untangling her mother's overnight knots. The daily ritual both soothed and irritated. Mary loved her mother, and willingly gave this time daily. Mary understood some biology and the care she offered her mother had answered a few questions, important now as she herself had had her first menstruation, but still, confusion reigned. At school she watched on silently as other girls chatted and giggled.

Releasing the hairbrush, she stroked her hands down both sides until they reached her hips. She softly stroke her body, going upwards across her stomach, touching her breasts, as if in a trance. A cough sounded along the hall, breaking the spell. Her eyes flew open and she felt foolish. She waited, but no more sounds came, and she returned to the brushing, as her earlier thoughts melted away.

Stuart's removal from Chancery School had been more positive than he could have anticipated. Yes, the experience had been painful and his relationship with his parents had suffered, but his new school, Rushmore Comprehensive, seemed a world away. While Chancery's appeared austere and full of tradition, Rushmore was engaging and the atmosphere was pleasant, a welcome change. There were still bullies, of course, and Stuart knew there always would be, but as far as he could tell, the staff took a firm stand against it.

Over the winter and on through spring, he'd held onto his job in the village store. Phil Riley even trusted him enough to manage the place for a few hours. Occasionally there would be the odd awkward moment as a gossip would arrive, or worse, Paul, though so far his luck had held with Phil close to make sure customers couldn't make a nuisance of themselves.

Overall, there wasn't much to complain about and the extra ten minutes cycle time meant he stood taller and leaner than he'd ever known. Only, he couldn't stop thinking about Mary. He'd been back to the farm a few times, though in early January a shout erupted from a hulking figure in their yard, causing Stuart to bolt away to safety. Nothing came of it but the scare was enough to put him off. Beyond the occasional glance as she passed by on the school bus, they seemed destined to be apart. He wondered, what if she missed him as much as he missed her? He hoped they'd be back in touch but for now, he had a new circle of friends, albeit none from the village, and was doing well in school.

He examined the Easter egg his parents had given him. The chocolate egg appeared average. The hollow shell opened up to reveal a tiny bag of chocolate beans. Stuart prodded with his index finger, counting fourteen in all. He sighed, disappointed. Earlier there were five such eggs on the dining room table. His parents had made it plain he should only take one, and that meant his younger sister would have the rest. He didn't begrudge his sibling, though he felt she'd guzzle the lot, resulting in chastisement for her gluttony. No, he resented the ongoing punishment. He resented that they didn't believe him. But Daisy, who was just under ten, was thrilled when she saw the pile of eggs. By then Stuart had vanished back to his room, with a smaller egg. Deciding fourteen chocolate beans weren't worth bothering with, Stuart went outside.

A chilly early mist had dissipated, leaving glorious blue skies and an intense warming sun. Stuart walked down the garden, ignoring his bike, and on out through the gate at the back. Content to drift like the few remaining clouds, he set out across the fields, barely registering where he was heading, and it didn't take long before he strode along the bridle path. He recalled his sprint, two years earlier, as he'd tried and failed to keep up with Paul's fleeing form. The temperature felt too warm for running, though he knew he'd manage the run easily now. All the deliveries and the resultant bike rides had seen his fitness levels improve drastically. There would be no sweaty palm print against the brickwork while his chest heaved in protest today.

He ambled onward through the trees until he came to the gate and Hunter field beyond. Someone had replaced the tether with a sturdy bolt, though part of the lower gate still showed signs of the kicking it had received. Stuart looked out across the grass. The meadow looked inviting, with its blanket of yellow and white flowers. Today, no sheep grazed. Stuart remembered recent signs inviting villagers to a lambing open day. He supposed the sheep and their offspring would be closer to the farm. Ahead lay the stream, which in the warm day looked inviting. After removing his socks and trainers, he sat dangling his toes in the icy water. It sent a jolt up his spine. Within seconds, he closed his eyes and the tentative dip became a full immersion. He reclined fully, not caring how much dust would cover the back of his shirt. The position felt comfortable with the sun beating down across his face and his ankles swirling in the stream.

Just as he was fully relaxed, he heard a gentle thud. His eyes sprang open, only to shut immediately as the sunlight stung his retinas. Grabbing a metal rail which ran along the side of the bridge, he hauled himself upright. Stuart pulled his feet out of the water and rested them on the side. They'd get dirty, but that didn't matter. Blinking repeatedly, he searched for the source of the noise. A figure approached, dancing lightly across the grass. He shook his head in disbelief; it was Mary. She clearly hadn't seen him yet, and panic set in. It had been ages since he'd seen her. What was he to do? For a moment he considered making a dash for cover, before realising just how foolish he'd look, running across the grass barefoot; anyway, she'd be sure to see. Too late, she'd spied him. He looked on, despairingly, expecting her to turn and flee. She didn't. Her pace slowed and she eyed him cautiously. She seemed to head even closer.

He offered a gentle wave, convinced he must look an idiot. Her result surprised him. It appeared her stride had lengthened as she drew closer.

'Hi,' she offered brightly.

'Sure,' he offered. As soon as the words had left his mouth, he berated himself. He gripped the railing to stop an obvious shake, but it was no good. He knew he was gawping. She didn't seem to mind.

'Are you going to nudge up, or are you planning on hogging the entire stream?'

Stuart shuffled along, convinced he was dreaming. Mary stood alongside and, using the rail for balance, she took off her own trainers and socks before setting down beside him. He just looked on, stunned.

She let out a little squeal as her toes dipped and then the pair settled side by side in silence. He could feel his chest pounding. Despite the tranquillity of the situation, Stuart could not remember ever having felt so tense. The water chill distracted him at least.

Without notice, she kicked gently out, causing a small splash upon his shin. He turned, perplexed.

She offered him a big smile.

This was new. This was something wonderful and unexpected. He'd seen her smile and dreamed of this moment, yet everything had been at a distance or within his head. Now, as his brain finally caught up, he realised she was there, and she was pleased to see him.

'Shall we start again? Hi.'

'Hi.'

Stuart recalled how when they'd originally worked on their Christmas assignment together, how, once he'd overcome his nerves, their connection had been amazing. She was offering a connection again, and he wasn't about to refuse.

'It's so nice to see you. Do you come here often?' Damn, another corny line.

'No, well, not as often as I like. I love it on a day like this. What about you?'

Stuart recalled the horrible day when Paul set about the sheep and shuddered, though he pretended the cold water caused the reaction. 'No, I haven't been down here in a long while. I do like it here and I'm really glad you came along.'

'Do you mean that?' she asked.

He could see she was earnest. 'Yes, of course. There is only one thing I missed when I left Chancery's and that was you. I know I screwed up, and you were right to let rip at me. I helped the bullies, and I was part to blame. I have many regrets about that day.'

'I do too,' she whispered.

Her response threw Stuart. Why would she feel regrets? She had done nothing wrong. His furrowed forehead must have suggested this.

'I told you I never wanted to talk to you ever again, before I knew all the facts.'

'It's ok. I know I played my part with that stunt they pulled on poor Liam. I mean, it surprised me. There was no way I could have known what they planned, but I let it happen.'

Mary reached her arm around Stuart's waist. 'I'm not sure you did anything wrong. They caught you in the moment, leaving you stuck between two brutish friends, trapped. They engineered it all. Look at everything which happened in the months afterwards? You stepped away from them.'

'Yeah, not that it did me much good,' he replied sullenly.

Her grip around his waist tightened and, feeling a flourish of happiness, he wrapped his own arm around her and pulled her closer. They sat in silence, each strangely comfortable in this new scene.

When they realised their feet had become ice cold, they quickly got up. Two pairs of wet footprints now stood on the bridge. They faced each other and Stuart's heart started racing, flowing faster than the stream below. He reached out, and she rewarded him by mirroring the gesture. His eyes moved up, taking in every detail of her exquisite form, until they rested upon her angelic face. Her fingers, interlinked in his, squeezed and he took that as permission to do what he'd always dreamed of. Carefully, in case he'd misread the situation, he cupped one hand behind Mary's neck and drew her in until their lips brushed. She offered no resistance, and he kissed her.

The kiss was clumsy; he felt sure, and he broke away, desperate to see her reaction. She didn't seem to mind; her eyes shone like the sunlight within the water.

'Wow,' he finally croaked. 'I've wanted to kiss you for such a long time.'

Her smile lit up. 'We are funny, aren't we? I missed you when they forced you out of our school and now here we are. Maybe being together is fate.'

Stuart's head spun. Things this good never happened to him. A new, adventurous feeling flowed through him. He wanted to blurt out he loved her, to shout from the treetops and tell the world.

Could he, should he? A cacophony of thoughts and emotions bombarded him, swiftly followed by doubts and insecurity. It must have shown.

'It's ok. I feel the same,' she offered, squeezing his hand.

Her comfort helped, though Stuart still struggled. He wanted to bottle this day up and keep it forever, yet felt sure he'd ruin things somehow. Bucking against his thoughts and fears, he thought of other people in his life trying to figure what they would do in his shoes. It didn't take him long to know the answer. He'd dispelled his parents and sister and even school friends. His answer came when he considered his time at the shop. Phil Riley had shown him many times to be positive and put trust in other people.

'You are amazing,' he smiled.

She blushed, and led him, walking barefoot across the grass, careful to avoid thistles or dung patches. The soft meadow felt warm between their toes, the daisies and buttercups encapsulated their mood perfectly. It *was* perfect. The sun continued to beat down, so he gently pulled her towards some dappled shade. He kissed her again, and enjoyed the feel of her warm body against him.

'What's it like up on your farm? We hardly ever see you down in the village,' he asked.

A whirlwind of emotions crossed Mary's face. At first, fleetingly, there was a look of fear; then a mask of assurance that didn't quite convince and finally an expression of realisation as she said: 'It was you who came to our farm that time, wasn't it? Were you spying on us?' She sprang up.

Stuart stumbled backwards, suddenly unsure of himself. He'd trespassed and now she knew it. Her eyes grew wide and the fear he'd seen earlier returned. Before he could work out what was going on, she darted off back to the bridge, slipped on her trainers and sprinted back across the field. Within seconds, she had gone.

Dumbfounded, Stuart put on his shoes and walked back home. He dragged his feet, constantly scuffing the tips of his trainers, but he didn't care. He'd ruined a beautiful moment, and he could've kicked himself. Why had he gone and spied on Mary? Ruined it all, as usual?

Back at the farm, Mary crashed through the kitchen door in a breathless clump. She didn't care who saw. The room stood empty, and she rushed over to the sink. Her chest heaved and a sharp acid taste lingered at the back of her throat. It tasted vile. Her whole body shook, and she almost vomited. Slowly, the feeling subsided, allowing her to take a sip of water. The cool liquid took away the bitter taste, though immediately it transported her back to the stream, causing her to spit it out in disgust. She couldn't do this, not anymore. She'd wanted her moment with Stuart for so long and now everything lay in tatters.

Storming upstairs, she launched herself into her bedroom, where she remained for the rest of the day. Keith would have to do his own sodding jobs.

Chapter Sixteen

PAUL COULDN'T PUT HIS finger on when it had happened, but he knew Harry had taken over control. A year earlier, everything had been clear. He was the boss, and he called the shots. With Paul as the brains, everything had worked. Now bloody Eddie Dyer and Bruno Chambers adhered themselves to Harry and he was hanging on behind, unable to figure out how to flip things into his favour. As a group, they were formidable, and their number added to their strength; only three of them lived together, and Paul was miles away, out on his own.

Looking out of his window, he felt miserable. Despite the glorious weather, there had been no plans for a meeting with Daley, and he felt sure the others had gone into Oxford without him. A movement in the distance caught his eye. Whoever the figure was, they were too far off, though he knew the bridle path and it seemed they were running. A smile formed as recognition hit. It was Mary. Something appeared to have spooked her, and she looked to be heading for home. Forgetting his other concerns, Paul dragged his trainers out from underneath his bed and set off to intercept.

Outside, Paul walked forward, expecting to see her at any moment. He didn't know how their conversation would go. *What would he say?* Turning into the lane, he cursed as he realised he'd misjudged her pace. He briefly considered turning about, though what was the point? He'd only return to mope in solitude. Deciding he had enough of that, he marched on, hoping to find Mary alone.

The main gate to the farm stood open, and he walked through. Nobody shouted or came to greet him, so he pushed on. The estate felt stale, though he'd never visited before, and his curiosity overrode his concerns. Tall metal buildings loomed to one side, offering a small amount of shade, and there before him lay the farmhouse. Deciding he'd just go for it, he found the front door and held his fist up, ready to knock. That would be the right thing to do, in case her parents were about, though after letting his eyes sweep the area, he went in unannounced.

The front door opened, and he stepped through. Instantly, Paul was on full alert. She had to be inside; he was certain, but where were the others? Before him lay a long hallway with stairs to the left. Two rooms flanked the corridor; closed doors were all he could see as he peered down into the gloom. Stepping left, he tried a handle. It turned easily, but Paul hadn't expected the door to scrape loudly. He hastily shut the door, waiting for everything to lapse into silence once more. Although wary of his intrusion, Paul felt excitement as he tried the door opposite. This one opened smoothly, but yielded nothing beyond dusty piles of junk. That left ahead or upwards. Again, he listened intently while trying to figure where Mary would be. With no idea of the building's layout, he had to assume she'd passed the corridor. He moved forward silently across the tiled floor, heading towards the back of the farmhouse. With each room he mentally ticked them off as empty, acknowledging a door out through the kitchen and French windows at the rear. Still, no sounds came to his ears.

He paused and considered whether he could have been wrong. Maybe the figure running hadn't been Mary, but someone else. After all, he'd lost sight of her as soon as he'd left home. Maybe her home was empty? He pondered the idea. He knew he should just walk away, but something drew him on. His plan had been to catch her. What then, he did not know, but if he couldn't frighten her today, then maybe he could take something or leave a message. Yes, that was it. Set her up and make her scared. The fledgling idea took on shape as he stepped back towards the staircase.

Taking the first step, he felt his foot sink a little. Paul lifted back up before a creak could sound and moved his foot closer to the side. Steadier now he moved upward, listening all the time. Each stride took him further away from the safety of the front door exit, yet Paul didn't care. He enjoyed the thrill of a mission. With each step, his confidence grew along with his pace, though a groan emitted when he finally stepped out onto the landing carpet. Like an agent from mission impossible, he spied the floor, theatrically imagining tripwires and mines. No other sounds came, so he set off down the landing to see who or what he could find.

The first bedroom stank and Paul recoiled without even attempting any inspection. The room sat in darkness, which Paul seemed happy to leave behind. Ahead lay a second bedroom with the door ajar. Here, a fluttering shadow caused him to be more cautious. Peering through, he could see a curtain sway in a feeble breeze. A noise caught his ear. The sound of breathing. He stopped moving, though his heart seemed to pound out of his chest with the volume of an orchestra. Could Mary be in there, resting just on the other side of the door? He could look at her. He could touch her. The thrill seeped into his entire being and he stepped fully into the room.

Immediately, he realised he'd read the situation horribly wrong. On the bed lay a woman, wrapped snugly in white sheets. She appeared to be asleep but something about the woman's face seemed wrong. The cogs in Paul's brain seemed to have ground to a stop as he tried to process it. All the excitement he'd felt seconds earlier had gone, only to be replaced with anxiety. Before he could properly process the scene, a shriek erupted close to his ear. The sound snapped him out of the stupor and he spun around.

Mary stood in the doorway, her face a mask of rage. Her screamed message was simple.

'Get out. Now!'

Paul sat at the back of the school bus as usual. Often the driver would leave without Mary, meaning she'd arrive an hour late for school. Not today, though, and Paul bit down on his thumbnail when he saw her slim figure approach. 'Shit,' he cursed.

Throughout his remaining holiday, he'd fretted over his visit to her home. He had no excuses. Who was the woman and why hadn't she stirred when Mary let rip her scream? He found it unsettling. Had the woman been breathing? He wasn't sure. Maybe she was dead. There was certainly something wrong with her face.

Now, back on the bus and seeing Mary, the thought returned to kick his gut. Had he seen a dead woman upstairs on the farm? He remembered the stench from one of the other rooms. Christ, there could be a room full of bodies up there. He shuddered at the idea. Despite the bullying he'd done at school, this took things to a whole new level. Feeling uneasy, he considered himself lucky to get out of there.

The journey seemed tedious, though as far as Paul could tell, Mary hadn't glanced his way even once. That suited him. He still hadn't got his head around things. On the one hand, it was her word against his, unless the police became involved and started dusting for prints. He hoped that was an absurd idea. Talking to Harry and the others wouldn't help either. Even talking with Daley seemed out. He could talk to his teacher, of course, though not about this, not in school at any rate. In the end, he decided to leave it.

Mary felt the sickness building as she climbed aboard. Her stomach cramped and churned noisily. She knew he'd be there, lurking. She remembered the day that Paul had invaded her domain. Were Paul and Stuart alike? It was a ghastly thought. She'd screamed until her lungs felt they would burst. Even her dad had woken. As usual, Graham Fortune's response was merely a slurred shout of Keith's name before rolling back into his room. Paul had galloped down the stairs and out of the front door before her father could utter any kind of protest. All the while, Mary had stood, her entire body shaking.

Somewhere on the bus, a weird buzz sounded, snapping Mary back to the present. Bobbie Wall sat two rows back with headphones planted across both her ears. Strains of "Do you want to hurt me?" echoed down the aisle. With little choice, Mary closed her eyes and drank in the lyrics. The words resonated. She liked the song and leaned to one side and back, to hear more clearly. When the song finally ended, she felt disappointment, though the next track sounded just as good. As the bus finally stopped to disgorge the pupils, Mary dived off quickly and stepped away. She sought a tree to hide behind, with two things on her mind. Paul stepped off seconds later.

He looked about, shrugged and set off towards the main building. Her breathing eased as he disappeared.

Bobbie followed seconds later, with earphones jiggling around her neck. The girl seemed engrossed in her copy of *Smash Hits* magazine, despite being buffeted from behind as others clambered off the bus. Mary watched, captivated to see the bright pop stars plastered across the cover. She only knew a little about Bobbie. As she watched, Mary wondered how to get closer to the girl. She wasn't sure what lay inside the magazine; a world of glamour seemed to invite her in.

Simmons watched the school corridors swell with a feeling of dread. Was this going to be another term starting with a blackmail note? *Where were the demands?* He taunted himself again. The Easter holidays had allowed no escape. He'd rowed with Molly before a quick break to Dorset and in the end, his wife had travelled down alone. He knew something had to give, otherwise he'd be heading for the divorce courts.

He returned to his office to seek his trusty drinks cabinet.

'Ah, Ms Tavistock, is the head in? I'd like a word?'

The school secretary looked up from her desk and smiled warmly at Daley.

'Yes, he is in there, Roger, though I'm not sure he wants to see anyone. You know how he gets.' Una Tavistock lowered her voice. 'I think he's been drinking... again.'

Daley returned the smile with equal warmth. He had no desire to get off with the hag, and being called 'Roger' by her filled him with unease, but Simmons drinking too much during school hours was information he could use. He feigned shock.

'Again,' he spluttered. 'Are you saying our head has a drinking problem?'

Daley watched the secretary's face change as the woman weighed up how much to reveal.

'You know, I think just maybe he has.'

Daley adjusted his face until it radiated an appropriate mix, showing sternness tempered with sympathy. Here sat an ally he could cultivate.

'Maybe I'll leave the head alone for now. Though I am worried.' Daley took a step back and straightened his tie before continuing. 'I don't want to sound presumptuous, but would you like to have dinner with me sometime? I'd like to get to know you better and maybe we could both offer support to Mr Simmons. I'm sure between us we could find a group that supports alcoholics.'

Choosing the word "alcoholic" had been a gamble. He wanted her on board and he needed to plant the seed of Simmons being incapable of running his school.

Her gushing reply came immediately. 'Well, that is a surprise. Of course, I'd love to have dinner with you, Roger.'

Once he'd stepped out of the office, Daley smirked. His bluff in the second letter, threatening to reveal Simmon's secret, had paid off. Much better to use drunken incompetence as a way to get rid of Simmons than raking up the other information that was also part of his own past...

Chapter Seventeen

Despite seeing Mary on the school bus every day, Paul decided by the end of the first week back, he was safe. She had said nothing to him. His confidence returned, and with it, his bullying persona.

He sought Eddie and Bruno, deciding not to include Harry but he was out of luck as all three stood together near a feeble first year who looked terrified.

'Come on. I won't say it again. Lunch money, now.'

Paul looked on, wondering if the kid was about to pee his pants. A few silver coins clattered on the floor; the kid was shaking. Paul had seen enough. He wanted to talk to his mates, so he advanced quickly and barged into the youngster, causing him to fall to his knees.

'Nice one, Paul. We wondered when you'd show up. As you can see, we're keeping busy making sure the runts pay up.'

'It's the sodding bus. I'm not lucky like all of you. I have to travel in each day.'

'Why don't you move, you stupid wanker?' Eddie chimed.

The others laughed.

'Come on. You know I'm stuck in the bloody village that died. Christ, it's so boring.'

'Yeah, I bet you bore everyone who lives there.'

The dig from Harry hurt, though Paul offered a raucous laugh to deflect, followed by scooping up the coins from the floor. 'Now piss off, you little shit,' he said as their victim scuttled away. 'Here you go,' he continued as he handed the cash over.

Harry's mouth widened to reveal several black fillings. 'Ta. We're heading into town on Saturday. You want to tag along?'

'Sure. What's the plan?'

'Thought we'd check out the new arcade,' Harry laughed while waving the coins under Paul's nose. 'Then we'll have a little cruise around and have some fun.'

Paul knew the arcade would be an expense he couldn't afford, though clearly the others looked flush. Before they could make any arrangements or he could mock their idea of cruising, the bell sounded to summon them all to class.

At lunch, Mary sat alone as usual. She kept an eye out for Bobbie. The clock clicked down and once half the break time had gone, Mary accepted she had to do something. She looked around and soon spotted her. Like Mary, Bobbie sat alone. She ambled over.

'Hi,' she offered, before realising the headphones and bouncing head meant Bobbie hadn't registered. She moved across until her shadow fell upon the girl, who looked up. Shock at the intrusion registered, swiftly followed by a flicker of irritation, though this quickly vanished. Bobbie clicked the stop button and looked up expectantly.

'Yes?' the girl asked dryly.

'Oh, I was wondering what you are listening to? I picked up some earlier when we were on the bus together, which sounded fab.'

'Just playing the Top Forty. My brother can be lame, but he has his uses. He records it for me every Sunday.'

Mary nodded, curious. Nobody ever switched on their television or radio at home. Her meagre cultural knowledge came from the violent songs and posters in Keith's room. Sometimes her brother played music he called metal at a volume loud enough to rattle the windows. Bobbie's music seemed so much lighter, more fun.

'Can I have a listen?'

The girl considered the request before nodding, so Mary settled down alongside and leaned in. The play button nudged down and Bobbie returned to her head, bopping, while Mary listened in awe. As the song played, it moved onto a chorus and Bobbie started singing along.

'Come on, sing along.'

Slowly, Mary learned the rhythm. As she sang, she knew her words lagged, but it didn't matter. The song about some woman called Eileen got to her.

'Wow,' she said finally, once the song had finished.

'Yeah, it's one of the best. Here, have a look at this.'

Mary gawped at the glossy pictures as they flicked through the magazine. It was incredible. She'd never seen or heard anything like it. It must have shown as Bobbie offered a weird look, but the bell sounded before either could react.

Together, they walked across the grass to class. Mary chatted excitedly while Bobbie nodded and smiled.

Roger Daley stared at himself in the mirror before heading out with a contented smile plastered upon his face. The idea of a date with

Una Tavistock held little appeal but he hoped the food and wine would help him get through the evening. He'd booked the restaurant, an inexpensive brasserie, for early in the evening. He shuddered at being stuck with her late at night.

The drive to collect her went smoothly, though his nervousness returned as soon as she stepped out of her front door. *She's gone crazy*, he thought, shocked. Instead of the straight, lifeless hair she wore to the school, a riot of curls, held together by a large red bow, sat up and flopped about in the breeze. The effect amplified the woman's head, but she hadn't stopped there. A clutch of lime green and pink bangles jangled up one arm almost to the elbow, gigantic hoop earrings, and a black dress with see-through frills completed the outfit. She looked like a woman desperate to come across younger. She failed miserably, Daley thought grimly. He'd not dressed up but wore his usual suit and tie. She stood at her gate, waving energetically, while he looked on aghast. Slack jawed, he sat still. Once it became apparent he wasn't moving, she scuttled over.

This would not be as easy as he first hoped. Leaning over, he waggled the door handle until it swung open.

'Oh, this is exciting,' she declared. 'I can't remember when I last went out on a date. So are you going to Roger me, Roger?'

Had Daley been drinking, he'd have spat the liquid across the dashboard, but as it was, he suppressed a dry cough while starting the engine. 'Let's see how dinner goes, shall we?'

During the twenty minutes it took to drive into Oxford, chatter poured out and Daley could only find relief by concentrating on the roads while she wittered on. Even when they finally found a parking space, her mouth only paused while he got out and walked around to open her door. Daley quelled the urge to run by repeatedly reminding himself this was merely an information-gathering exercise.

'Come on, it isn't far to walk,' he said gruffly.

'Hang on, Roger, what's the hurry? I thought we'd take a stroll by the river first.'

Daley paused. This wasn't the plan. They'd half an hour until their booking time and he thought that time would be filled by a pint or two.

'Will you be alright walking in those? You looked unsteady earlier, and it is quite a way down to the water, especially when we haven't much time.'

'Aw, I knew you cared. Don't worry, silly. As long as you hold my arm, I won't fall, except maybe into you,' she snorted.

Like a man condemned, Daley began the walk towards the river.

The woman clung on to Daley, her tight grip adding to his discomfort. Within the confines of the car, he'd noticed her strong perfume, and now, as she pressed herself firmly to his side, the smell became overpowering. He turned his face away, hoping she wouldn't notice, though before long her arm pulled him tighter and he forced a limp smile in her direction.

'There you are, Ms Tavistock,' Daley declared when they finally arrived at the Thames. Her grip slackened and she stepped away slightly.

'Now then, Roger, it's Una and you well know it. Come on, there's a bench, we can cuddle up.'

Nobody led Daley, certainly not since his own school days at least. Used to being the dominant party, he flailed ineffectively as she dragged him to the seat. Checking his watch proved difficult as she refused to relinquish control of his arm. His backside shuffled awkwardly while she jabbed her finger animatedly, pointing at a duck swimming by. He suppressed the urge of taking the fowl and stuffing it down Ms Tavistock's throat. Maybe then he could get a word in.

Finally, the ducks swam away. Clearly, all the woman's waving had seen them off. Daley coughed and when she ignored the subtle message, he tugged her arm before suggesting they head to the restaurant. The path back into the city took longer as a section of cobbles took some negotiating. Daley was sure she'd engineered the route as she kept stumbling. Three times he caught her and prevented a fall, and each time her eyes glinted in delight. He wasn't sure he could keep the pretence up much longer as the idea of dropping her and heading home appealed. With each wobbly step, Daley weighed up the risks of letting her drop...

Paul's trip to the arcade had been a disaster. The other three, fresh from raiding the first year's lunch money, came loaded while he had ten measly pounds, which his mum had given him to buy new trainers. Christ, he couldn't get anything decent for that, especially since he'd already broken into the note to pay for his bus fare. When he finally arrived, they were nowhere to be seen. So much for a meet-up with friends. He knew where they would be, pissing their stolen gains up the wall and sure enough, he could see Harry's bulky form through the window of the arcade. Jesus! His mate looked bigger than the Donkey Kong game he leant against. Beyond him, Eddie jostled with a joystick, making it seem easy to leap over piles of animated barrels. Just as Eddie looked certain to complete another level, Harry gave him a shove, which brought the game to a swift halt.

Paul felt uneasy as he reached for the door and walked in.

'Hey, Paul. We wondered where you'd got to. Come on, we've been here ages and Eddie's taking the piss with the scores he's racking up. How about you have a go?'

Paul looked at Harry and then at the others. Maybe it was his imagination, but something close to a sneer seemed to flick across Harry's face, though in an instant the look had vanished, replaced instead with flat lips, covered by bright flickering from a myriad of coloured lights.

'Sure. What are we playing?'

The other three laughed in unison before pointing inanely at the machine they'd been using. 'What else? Think you can beat our resident Donkey Kong champ?'

Paul pushed past Bruno to examine the machine. He'd played a similar game once before at the swimming baths, but that had been all about collecting pills in a maze. As the others looked on, he wished he'd stayed outside. At least, then he could watch and learn how to play the dammed thing.

'Come on, we haven't got all day. Are you playing or not?'

Paul listened as his coin fell through the slot to settle into a money box behind before thumping the red start button. A little animation played, showing a huge gorilla, and then the game began. He figured out how to move sideways and up and down quickly enough, but failed miserably by jumping at all the wrong times instead of over the obstacles. In under a minute, his game ended with nothing to show for it except a slightly lighter pocket and heckles of ridicule from his so-called mates. After much jeering and four more equally awful games, he stepped away to give Bruno a go. His friend fared only slightly better, though Bruno held a fistful of coins and came away unscathed from any teasing. Next, Eddie took a turn. He was a natural, and Paul could feel his face twisting in a grimace as the minutes ticked by, while Eddie's game character continued to survive. A small crowd of onlookers formed to highlight Eddie's brilliance. In the end, Eddie missed out on the highest score, though his three initials still stood proudly on the list showing the top players.

Together, the group played more games, though when Harry played and lost, nobody offered any ridicule. Paul tried to win on the slot machines that devoured pounds and gave little in return. The others had loads of cash, mashed in their sweaty palms, but while his friends' eyes flashed with greed, Paul veered closer to dismay upon feeling the empty cloth within his pocket.

When they moved to yet another machine, Paul raised his hands in defeat. 'Sorry boys, but that's me done. I'm all out of cash.'

Nobody spoke as Paul waited for the others to offer some money and bail him out.

'You'd best sod off then,' Harry snorted.

Paul looked across at Eddie and Bruno's sheepish faces as they merely shrugged.

'Thanks a lot,' Paul snapped back as he marched towards the exit. Before he could spill out onto the street, he looked back. Instantly, he regretted the action as he felt a stab of jealousy. Harry stood with Eddie and Bruno on either side, wrapping his beefy forearms around their shoulders in a tight hug. Nobody would be following. He thudded into the door. Outside, it took several seconds for his eyes and ears to settle. His watch read 5:48 p.m. Crap, not only had they wasted the entire afternoon, but worse, he'd lost all his money. Paul looked around as the shops showed signs of closing and let out a moan. Shit, he cursed. He knew he couldn't explain losing his money or why he hadn't bought a pair of trainers.

Plenty of shoppers mingled about. Paul stood in limbo, unable to return to the arcade, though equally reluctant to head home.

Something clanged, breaking the spell, and he moved off, keen to get away from any watchers in the arcade. Despite quickening his pace, he arrived just as his bus disappeared around a corner. Paul studied the timetable, and his mood soured more. He would have a thirty-minute wait.

Clouds hustled about overhead and as the shadows lengthened, Paul shivered. Looking about, he spied a low wall but he turned away in disgust as bird shit coated the entire surface. He smirked, remembering the look Harry had given him back in the arcade. His brain fired inventive plots where Harry became a victim. The notion appealed. With Harry out of the picture, Eddie and Bruno would fall back into line with him as leader.

He knew he couldn't act alone. He'd need Daley's support if he wanted to get rid of Harry. Just thinking about the teacher set Paul's mind racing. Confused thoughts intermingled with exquisite memories. Not that things between them were wrong. Oh hell, they weren't right either. He'd barely seen his mentor during the spring and now that he thought about it, he wondered whether they would ever have any time together again? Nah, they were good; they *had* to be. Paul shook his head, keen to dispel any doubts.

Then he saw them. At first he didn't recognise the gaudy woman wearing black with the many bangles on her arm, but there was no doubting Daley. Together, his teacher and the woman walked along the street opposite. They looked like a couple, his arm wrapped around her lovingly. As the woman wobbled on her heels, Daley seemed attentive and keen to save her from a fall.

Finally, he realised just who the woman was. Paul's mind crumbled at Daley's deception before he turned away in disgust.

Chapter Eighteen

MARY SAT ALONE, WRAPPED in the farm's stillness. It was like this sometimes, especially now Keith spent less time around. She couldn't bring herself to ask him where he went each day. Any question she'd dare to ask him would cause a swift rebuttal, or worse. Even her dad had gone. He'd staggered out of bed before stumbling downstairs. Earlier, her nose had wrinkled in disgust as she saw him urinating behind the barn. Grateful he'd disappeared, Mary looked about the kitchen before heading upstairs to check on her mum.

She'd seen her an hour earlier, and nothing had changed. The vacant eyes kept staring. Today they focused on a blank section of wall, and Mary wondered whether things would ever be any different. Did she even know Paul had invaded her bedroom?

After patting down the pillows, Mary left her mother. As she turned down the landing, she saw Keith's door, shut as usual, with its "DO NOT ENTER" sticker slapped across the wood. She wondered what secrets lay inside and suddenly decided to find out. She turned the handle, expecting resistance. Finding none, she pushed open and peered into the gloom. With detritus strewn across the floor, she had to shove the door hard before a gap opened wide enough for her to enter.

Tentatively, she took a step forward. Empty drink cans and packets of crisps formed a blanket across the floor, making her feet crunch with every step inside. The room was a tip. A sliver of light from the edge of the curtain shone through and Mary carefully moved to the window to allow more light in. Her heart pounded as she looked at the chaos strewn about before her. Along with the floor, Keith's bed had taken on a role of dumping ground. Weirdly, once her eyes adjusted, she could see there was some kind of order: one corner was used as a clothes dump and the space under the window seemed to be the food zone. Plates, cutlery, and mugs lined up in a weird parade. She recoiled as a selection of stains, including mould, coated every item. Even the bed hadn't escaped. With the top sheet missing, her brother slept on the bare, stain-covered mattress. Like father, like son, she thought bitterly.

Her eyes continued scanning. More clothes littered the floor opposite, though these seemed to be mainly rags. She tried to pull at the wardrobe door but something jammed and she gave up, afraid the unit would topple. The chest of drawers looked more interesting. A weird excitement gripped her as she continued her inspection. She thrilled at her audacity to go snooping. The top two drawers were empty. At the bottom drawer, she stopped. This one had been heavier and tougher to open, and when she did, her hand shot to her mouth.

After seeing Bobbie's *Smash Hits* magazine, Mary had thought herself world wise, but Keith's magazines offered a whole new world of information. Hoping to remain undisturbed, she settled down to read.

Stepping into the shop, Stuart could see Phil Riley busy as always, so he moved through to the back of the shop to collect and sort his deliveries. There were extra slots today, but keeping active helped to quell his other confused feelings.

'Morning, Stuart. How are you today?'

Stuart spun and chuckled inwardly. He might have known he wouldn't sneak past unnoticed. 'I'm ok, I guess.'

'I guess? That tells me you have things on your mind. Care to share?'

Stuart sat back and marvelled at his boss' perceptiveness. He felt a pang of guilt as he never seemed to return the kindness.

'Why are girls so confusing?'

'Now there's a question I wasn't expecting,' Phil sighed. 'I reckon you aren't talking about girls, but one girl in particular. Am I right?'

'How do you do that? I mean, you're right, but nobody else knows. It's a waste of time talking with mum and dad.'

'Well, you know me, son. I'm not one for judging. Why don't you tell me all about it?'

Stuart felt his face redden. Would he share his secret with Phil? He finally mumbled, 'It's Mary.'

'Yes, that figures. I think she likes you too, you know.'

Stuart's eyes went wide. 'Has she said something about me? When? What did she say?'

'Whoa. Hold your horses. She comes to the shop from time to time and yes, she has asked about you.'

Stuart fell backwards in surprise, though the counter halted his progress. 'Wow,' was all he managed.

'Now that we've figured you like her and she likes you, what's the problem?'

'She doesn't like me, though. She can't.'

'Come on, you're babbling. What happened?'

Telling Phil came as a relief and, before long, Stuart had explained what had happened in the meadow. His boss listened attentively.

'I can see how you'd get the wrong idea and you wouldn't be the first to have misunderstandings.'

'You think I misunderstood? What, that I'm to blame?'

Stuart's cheeks flushed again. He apologised immediately for his outburst.

Phil just smiled. 'No, that isn't what I'm saying at all, but it's good you are passionate about it. It means you care. What I'm saying is, you triggered something. Something which upset and frightened Mary.'

Stuart realised that he didn't really understand Mary.

'So, what do I do? I, I think she's amazing, but I can't get close to her, not without breaking things at least.'

'I tell you what. I'll let you in about her and the rest of her family, but you must promise me not to tell her I said anything. Maybe, then you'll see why Mary behaves the way she does.'

Mary stepped away from Keith's room, thrilled by her new-found courage. After craning her ear once more, she decided it was time to inspect the other room, her father's. The door opened easily and, as expected, she smelled a terrible stench. There was no doubting the cause. After all, she couldn't ever remember seeing her dad sober. The room appeared bright, which surprised her. She took a step inwards, relieved the extra light allowed her to navigate safely all the sickly stains clinging to the carpet in some horrible bog-like parody. A sadness gripped her as she wondered how any human could sink this low. Spongy, sticky carpet greeted her every step, but she *had* to know. Had to understand the reason for his drunkenness. Her breathing felt laboured as the pungent air fought against her. More rubbish littered the floor in a flow, which included the bed. Mottled stains seemed to cover every surface, the only exception being an enormous pile of cans and bottles, gleaming in an odd riot of colours which could almost be artistic.

With nothing to see under the bed, she moved to the wardrobe. She stood surprised as she stared at the pristine suits and shirts inside. Here, at least, was evidence of cleanliness and normality. A tear trickled down her cheek. Closing the wardrobe door, she turned her attention to an old dressing table. The design mirrored the one in her mother's room. A solitary chair sat underneath, probably the only item of furniture unscathed from all the debris. The unit held six drawers, three on each side, and Mary pulled each open.

Unlike the neat wardrobe, the drawers revealed a disgusting array of sticky rags which may have been clothes once, but looked ready for the bin. Even the charity shops wouldn't want these. She struggled to open the bottom drawer, as she tugged furiously at it. Suddenly, it popped open, disgorging its contents across the floor.

Mary gasped, involuntary drawing in some of the filthy air. She couldn't help it. Her surprise was too great. The whole drawer was filled with cash. She marvelled. She'd never seen so much money. In fact, apart from the grocery money she had never had any herself. A thought flashed through her head. What if she took some? He wouldn't miss it, would he? Stuffing most of the cash back in, she sealed the drawer shut while holding a small bundle of notes in her shaking hand. It was time to go. She had to keep her discovery secret. Closing the door, she stealthily returned to her room. She didn't know why she tiptoed across the landing; it might have been partly guilt. Safely inside her own bedroom, she exhaled deeply and sat, relieved, inspecting her loot. She counted fifty pounds, more money than she'd ever owned.

Daley stood at his sink and groaned. The sound of the water pouring into his glass set his head on edge. He'd drunk too much the previous evening, and he knew he shouldn't have driven after the meal. He had to, though. Within the confines of the dingy restaurant, Una Tavistock had fawned over him. Unconsciously, he felt his ankle, aware of how the woman had kicked him playfully under the table at dinner. There was sure to be a bruise. He knew he'd drunk excessively. *Anything to make the date bearable*, he thought bitterly. She'd been a willing accomplice. At one point she insisted they both work their way through an array of cocktails, each more lurid and vile than the last. Her eyes had beamed as umbrellas and other paraphernalia jutted out from each giant glass.

He glared at the Alka Seltzer, which frothed and bubbled noisily before pushing it away. Pain stabbed his forehead, but now he had a remedy. His stomach baulked at the measure and he wondered whether he would vomit. After a few dry heaves, he turned off the tap and shuffled over to a table and chair, where he sat and stared into the glass. He couldn't ever remember feeling this old. In his clouded state, he wracked his brain for anything useful he could use against the head. Instead, tawdry images of the school secretary tormented his senses. It was going to be a long day.

Chapter Nineteen

May 1983

THE ROOM WAS DARK, but that suited Paul. Gripping the bottle tightly, he poured a generous measure before sealing the cap and setting it to one side. His nose wrinkled as he took a sniff. The alien aroma was unpleasant, and he stared at the glass in the gloom for several seconds before taking a swig. He spluttered as the fire hit the back of his throat. *Christ, how could adults drink this stuff?* The second gulp also burned; he took it down in a single swallow with merely a shake of his head. By the third mouthful, he'd emptied the glass. Despite shaky hands, he poured a refill.

This time, Paul held the intense liquid up to his eyes, mimicking a crystal ball. Images flooded his mind: Harry, Stuart, his parents, kids he'd bullied, and finally Daley. A tear rolled down one cheek, which he wiped away with a forearm. A sob formed at the back of his throat, which he tried to choke back. He couldn't and as his cries became more intense, he felt the glass clatter to the floor. Despite the noise, nobody came.

It took a while before he regained any semblance of composure, but then, with steely resolve, he opened his first packet. Pills dropped out across the sheet. He didn't know what they were. He didn't care. Once he'd opened the other packs, blue, white and red pellets intermingled. All he could think about was the oblivion he desired. Next, he lowered himself to the floor, seeking the glass he'd dropped earlier. It sat tantalisingly out of reach underneath a sturdy set of drawers and his fingers clawed at air, just inches away. *Was that it? Has my plan become derailed before it even began?* Urgently now, an inner voice spoke to him. Dark encouragement flowed from somewhere within his subconscious and he whipped about, searching for a tool. Then he remembered he still had the bottle. What did it matter if he lost the glass? A taunting laughter echoed within his head. Unscrewing the top, he tried again, only this time a clutch of capsules sat upon his tongue. Before another voice could challenge his decision, he glugged back another shot. Feverishly now, he grabbed more pills until he'd filled half his fist. A few fell to one side as he stuffed them into his mouth. He carefully measured how much vodka to imbue. The intense warmth didn't seem to bother him now. Maybe the pills had diluted the liquid? All he knew was he no longer cared. Slowly, as the bottle emptied, the voice in his head, which had taunted him into this action, quietened. Slipping away, he hoped there would be no tomorrow.

Stuart remembered when the ambulance came as the siren blare woke most of the villagers. Many seemed happy to gossip. He was shocked to hear they had rushed Paul to the John Radcliffe Hospital. *Shit*. He thought he hated Paul, yet somehow now, all he could feel was pity and sadness. After checking he had cash and his bike lock, he set out for the long ride into Oxford.

As he peddled along the A40, he questioned the actions he was about to take. Would a hospital visit accomplish anything? Would they even let him in? What would he say? Despite his fitness, the ride seemed harder than usual.

Arriving at the hospital, he saw a problem. He wasn't sure what he expected, but the mass of buildings overwhelmed as he tried to figure where they'd taken Paul. The estate was enormous. Thirty minutes and several questions later, he arrived.

Stuart looked along the length of a long ward as he waited patiently at the nursing station to be allowed access. He felt a strong temptation to turn away, but before his fears could take hold, a nurse steered him down to Paul's bed.

'We have given him some medication to counteract the pills he took, and he's bound to be groggy after having his stomach pumped, so I expect he won't be very chatty. Very lucky, your boy. You're a good friend to come down here. I'm sure he will appreciate your visit. Just ten minutes, though. He needs his rest.'

Once the nurse departed, Stuart drew up a chair and sat alongside Paul's bed. It had been over six months since they'd last seen one another. So far, Paul hadn't noticed his arrival. Feeling uncomfortable, Stuart stood and poured a beaker of squash before offering it over. Slowly Paul's head turned, and both looked at the other, each with enquiring faces.

'What are you doing here?' Paul croaked.

Stuart shrugged. *Hell, he didn't know why himself.*

'How are you? You look like shit. Juice?'

A wan smile. 'Sure.'

Half the squash trickled down Paul's chin as he drank. Before the hospital gown could become saturated, Stuart reached over with a paper towel.

'There you go. We can't have anyone from Chancery's see you dribbling.'

Paul spluttered and thrust the drink to one side.

'Sorry. I guess you don't want to think about school right now.' Stuart saw he was right so didn't push it. 'You asked me why I'm here. I know this may sound weird, but I just wanted to see if you are ok. You know, after what happened.'

'What have they said? Is everyone talking about me?'

'There was an ambulance. Sirens, lights, the lot. So, yeah mate. People are talking. They always will, though. It's up to us whether we listen.'

'Shit, you're getting profound, aren't you?'

'What about you? Profound's quite a long word. When did you swallow a dictionary?'

Before he could answer, the nurse returned.

'Now, you two. I need to call a halt to your chatter. I said it would just be a few minutes and Mr Winters had been through quite an ordeal. I expect there will scarring on his stomach lining, so best we let him rest.'

Their protests fell on deaf ears as the woman chivvied Stuart out of the ward, with him promising to visit again when he could.

Mary exited the bus in a buoyant mood. Today she wasn't going to walk into a classroom, she'd travelled to Oxford. Today, she planned to meet with Bobbie. She needed a break and felt confident her mum would be ok alone for a few hours, as long as Keith didn't come back; he seemed prone to mysterious disappearances lately.

'Hi. Glad you made it.'

Mary spun. She could feel her face flushing as her new friend surprised her. Her jaw dropped. Bobbie looked unrecognisable. Bright pink and yellow hues covered both her cheeks while intense red lips glistened in the sunlight. It wasn't just the crazy make-up. A denim jacket paired with a pink rara skirt and a light blue headband completed the outfit. Even Bobbie's hair seemed more elaborate.

Mary swallowed hard and, looking down at her own drab garb, the doubts set in. How on earth could she compete with that? It must have shown.

'You okay?'

'Sorry, yes. I just looked at you and thought, wow.'

Bobbie beamed and performed a pirouette. 'Yes, I am fabulous, aren't I?'

Mary had to agree. Bobby really looked amazing.

'So, what are we doing then?' Bobbie asked.

Mary closed her eyes and said a quick prayer.

'I was thinking you could help me. You know, with a makeover.'

'Well, what are we waiting for? Cinderella, you shall go to the ball.'

Two hours later, the pair fell into Bobbie's bedroom to inspect their purchases. Make-up, sprays, gels and a host of accessories littered the bed. Mary had severely dented her money, but she didn't care. Bobbie had covered every wall in a glossy montage of pop posters. The effect looked stunning. Most she recognised and although she'd allowed plenty of room for new romantic bands, pictures of Adam Ant and Boy George took centre stage.

'Is it their make up or music you prefer?'

'Both. I love their songs. In fact, I love all the songs of everyone pictured in here, but those two are my faves. I love how they dress up and express themselves. I want to be like them.'

Mary nodded while Bobbie sorted their shopping into two piles.

'Are you sure it's ok for me to have this stuff? I'm not complaining, but it is all expensive. I take months to save up for a pile like this.'

'Remember what we spoke about earlier? You help me learn about this stuff and I help you with a few treats. We agreed, right?'

'Yeah, I know, I know, but it seems to be a lot.'

'Well, you'd best get started then. How about you put on some music and then you can turn me into a pop princess?'

A few sniggers later, Bobbie set a tape playing. They burst into laughter as something weird called "Snot Rap" burst out of the speakers.

'Yeah, maybe not that one,' Bobbie chuckled as she pressed fast forward. Next, Bowie's "Let's Dance" played.

'Much more my vibe,' Mary replied.

As the music played, Mary continued to giggle.

'Mary, will you keep still? The foundation is going everywhere.'

It took longer than it should with lots of breaks to wipe away smears so Bobbie could reapply make-up, but eventually Bobbie sat back.

'Are you ready?' she asked, holding a mirror tantalisingly out of reach.

Mary paused, wondering what image the mirror would reveal. Despite one of her favourite songs, "True" playing, she bit her lower lip to quell her uncertainty.

'Oi, don't do that, you'll smudge your lippy. You look gorgeous. Here, look.'

Mary froze while Bobbie leaned the mirror to one side. Her friend stood to place one hand on her shoulders. She could feel her body tremble as her friend drew the mirror closer. And there it was. Mary's jaw dropped at the transformation. She looked amazing.

It made an incredible impression on Mary. For the first time in her life, she cast aside the dowdy girl she saw within herself. For an hour she danced, she sang, as the pair clutched hairbrushes to mimic the acts, and finally stared in disbelief at her own transformation. Not only that, she had an actual friend. She hugged Bobbie.

Reality hit her. The make-up had to come off. She couldn't go home looking like that. Dressing down and wiping everything away hurt. Bobbie nagged her to keep it on, but Mary knew she couldn't share her home life. Not yet.

By the time she left, the sun sat low in the sky and Mary realised she'd overdone her day away. She couldn't help it. She'd just have to face the consequences. Deciding the next bus wouldn't drive past for almost an hour, she set out across the fields. Ascot Midden was the next village along, so she knew it wouldn't take too long.

Chapter Twenty

SIMMON'S STOMACH GROWLED NOISILY, making him wonder if he was getting an ulcer. Something wasn't right, he thought, rubbing his thinning scalp and pondered where his enemies lay. Certainly, Una Tavistock was one. He knew the busybody liked nothing more than to gossip.

Standing, he winced at the acid reflux hit. Taking a handkerchief from his breast pocket, he wiped the sweat from his forehead. He looked down, seeing only a pot belly, before sighing. His hand hovered over the decanter before pulling away. No, that wasn't helping. Looking down, he could see a visible shake. It started at the tips of his fingers and worked up along the length of his left hand. Gripping both hands together, he fought to steady himself before placing the shaky palm down on his desk. It took a while for the tremor to subside and Simmons felt grateful at the lack of interruptions. This wasn't the behaviour of someone in charge of a school. He knew everything had unravelled since his appointment as head. He made a decision. He couldn't alter the past, but he dammed well could influence the future.

Acting before his enthusiasm could wane, Simmons locked away the decanter and vowed to leave the drink alone. Next, he turned his attention back to listing his enemies.

An hour later, the stomach pains still hadn't eased. They were worse. Every time his mind came back to the threatening notes, he returned to the figure he'd seen running away from his house the previous autumn. That had to be a pupil, probably from his school, but he did not know who which left him increasingly frustrated. Even the bullying which had plagued the beginning of his tenure seemed to have eased, leaving fewer plausible suspects.

After setting Una Tavistock to one side and deciding she would have to go, Simmons went through the entire staff list. A couple of names stood out. He flagged Roger Daley and Barry Potts as candidates. On the surface, Daley had handled the Foster beating efficiently and certainly by stepping in he'd limited any potential damage to the school, but something niggled in Simmon's mind. As for Potts, Simmons felt his head of PE had an enormous chip on his shoulder. Maybe it was because many did not see physical classes as educational. Simmons didn't know and he couldn't understand why Potts would take his insecurities out on him. He was a big promotor of physical wellbeing. If Simmons had his way, he'd have the pupils working up a sweat more often. That way, they'd be less likely to be disruptive once the academic work began.

Leaving his enemies aside, now Simmons focussed in the opposite direction. This time, he wanted allies. Ignoring a previously arranged meeting, he placed a call to the chair of governors.

Outside of his office, Una Tavistock sat in quiet contemplation. Her date with Daley hadn't gone entirely to plan, but she had enjoyed their evening together. She hadn't really decided about the man. In the beginning, he'd seemed standoffish, but once the drink flowed, they'd had a good time. It had been a couple of years since she'd last been out. If only he hadn't kept talking about Simmons all the time. That sucked the romance out of the room. Not all though. She remembered kicking off her shoe so she could waggle her foot under the table, teasing him by slowly going up his leg. Una felt her cheeks flush as she remembered her brazen behaviour. It was out of character, but she didn't care. She fancied Roger Daley and had no qualms about showing it. It didn't matter who else looked on. Being off the shelf meant she wanted to shout about her man.

A buzz sounded, drawing her from her daydream. She looked across at the switchboard and saw Simmons was making an outside call. Without even thinking, she lifted her receiver and, after pressing one button, she silently joined the call.

The time spent with Bobbie had released something inside of Mary. She had an urge to play taped music like her friend, though that would require another trip into the city and more money. The idea of taking more didn't sit well. She wasn't sure if they would miss more money vanishing and was afraid of getting caught. It was a bitter pill, being treated as a skivvy all the time. For now, all she had was her single copy of *Smash Hits*, though she'd already read it from cover to cover twice. It seemed so unfair she couldn't put the poster up, but how would she explain its sudden arrival? She could say Bobbie gave it to her, she mused, though Keith would likely rip it down out of spite. Then again, did he ever go into her room? She hoped not. Apart from the magazine, her room held no secrets, but it was still hers. She felt a guilty pang as she remembered her recent intrusion of Keith's and their father's rooms and resultant theft.

Trying to remain positive didn't work, either. Bobbie's parents were so welcoming. Her mum had offered drinks and snacks before allowing them both unfettered access to Bobbie's bedroom. She hadn't even batted an eyelid upon seeing Bobbie's make-up. In fact, she went much further. When she saw Mary's transformation, she clapped her hands, marvelling at her appearance. Nobody had ever done that before. Even brushing her own mother's hair had lost its lustre. A job which used to feel close, safe and happy now felt dull.

She had another problem, which fuelled her miserable mood. While Keith continued to spend time away from the farm, her dad, Graham, had returned to former habits. She couldn't remember the last time he'd stepped out of his room. Mary couldn't recollect the last time she'd seen him. He'd certainly been quiet recently. Too quiet.

Her home was never completely silent. Just the age of the building saw to that, with creaks emanating from rickety floorboards along with air gaps against many of the doors. Even the taps in the kitchen rattled and shook while disgorging their liquid.

Mary refilled a jug and took it upstairs. Her mum was in her bedroom; today she'd climbed out of bed to stand and stare unblinkingly out of the window.

'Hi Mum,' she said before putting the jug on the dresser.

As expected, no recognition showed, so she reached around to offer a hug. Her mum felt cold, hardly surprising given the flimsy nightgown and the temperature of the room. Mary made a mental note to put some soup on the stove. Pulling gently, she encouraged her mother back to the bed and once she'd lain down, she tucked her in.

'Right, you stay there and get warmed up and I'll be back soon with something warm to eat.'

Switching on a bedside lamp, she ran a hand through her mum's hair before heading back out of the room. Outside on the landing, she slumped against a wall, saddened as always. Her mother never left the farm and there was scant sound or colour to be found anywhere. Mary thought about the music she'd just encountered along with the make-up with its riot of colour. It wasn't just unfair she had to hide these new things from her father and Keith. Her mother missed out, too. Mary recalled her biology teacher speaking about the importance of stimulus. She added it to the ever-lengthening list of unfair problems.

Despite feeling despondent, Mary rallied, knowing she'd made a promise to cook food to her mum. Most kitchen cupboards were empty, though there were a couple of tins of tomato soup at least. The flavour didn't matter, she'd need to spoon it into her mum's mouth as always. Once the saucepan came to the boil, Mary gently decanted the steaming liquid into a bowl, which she placed on a tray ready to carry upstairs.

Taking care to avoid the spongy carpet on the third step, she climbed, but despite her care, the soup still slopped out onto the tray.

'Damn,' she cursed as she sat the tray down on the top step. She'd seen Keith leave hours earlier and didn't expect him back. That just left her dad. His room lay just a few metres away and today the door stood ajar. She didn't know what made her do it, but Mary stood and walked towards the opening. She'd become accustomed to the smell, but today something else mingled in the air. The entire room smelt unnaturally of decay. As her head snuck further into the room, she saw her dad lain prone in a sideways skew across the bed. She detected no signs of breathing but was sure he'd be drunk as usual.

Suddenly, she froze. Mary could feel her heart beating through her chest as she tried to decide what to do. Her body refused to move. She just stood, staring. Something flitted across her vision, bringing her back to the present. She watched as shadows hid the bluebottle for a moment, but then the insect settled upon her father's cheek. Graham didn't flinch or swat the intruder away and the fly remained as though staking claim to the space.

Mary stared, eyes unblinking. The tiny insect remained and with each passing second, her fears grew. She knew what she'd wished for. Had it happened? Taking a mechanical step forward, she let out a low groan. Only sightless eyes greeted her. This was not some drunken stupor. Her father, Graham Fortune, was dead.

'Roger, er... Mr Daley.' The shout rang out across the hall. It made him cringe. He turned, though he already knew the owner.

'Yes? How can I help you?' he hissed as pupils swarmed around. Most walked away, though a few children sniggered at the intrusion. His eyes narrowed as Una Tavistock scuttled forward to seize his attention.

'Roger. Oh, I'm so glad I found you,' she gasped.

Seeing a captive audience, he drew her into an empty classroom, closing the door behind them. Already he knew the smirking gossip mongers would create a problem, but at least now they had some privacy. Griping both her arms, he led her to a desk and pressed her into a chair. He could see she was flustered. Inwardly he sighed. *Better try honey.*

'Una, darling. You can't accost me in the corridor like that. Not with staff and students about.'

The fawning went unnoticed as her stammered reply reported the phone call she'd overheard. That Simmons wanted to get rid of her. Daley's mood transitioned from shock to joy but he quickly masked that expression and showed concern instead. He paced silently as he gathered his thoughts. The door had a small window, so he checked they were still alone. Outside appeared empty, so he moved across and clasped both of her hands, pulling her upright. From there, he drew her into a gentle hug, though once her head sat upon his shoulder, he looked beyond. His eyes looked out beyond the window, his mind was elsewhere. A plot formed. One where he used her knowledge of Simmons' drinking and then, as soon as her usefulness ended, he would grease any wheels he could to get her out of the school.

Stuart, along with most of the village, noted the sirens when they came. Unlike a few days ago, today the vehicle, with its flashing lights and noise, shot beyond the village and up the hill. Stuart's eyes went wide. He knew where it was heading. Seconds later, he'd mounted his bike and set off in pursuit.

Despite his fitness, his breath heaved when he cycled up to the farmhouse. But he had to know Mary was safe. The ambulance stood silent and empty. Stuart guessed they'd dashed inside and his fear returned. He threw his bike to one side and recklessly ran into the building. Hearing voices upstairs, he charged onward, calling Mary's name as he bounded upwards.

He expected pandemonium, but he spied two paramedics covering a body with a sheet while Mary looked on. She looked composed until her head turned and she saw him. Then something strange happened. She reached out with both arms, imploring Stuart to hold her. He stepped forward and drew her into his grasp. He didn't know what had happened, but at that moment, he didn't care. Mary was safe, which was all that mattered.

Later that day, the police arrived, though after talking to the ambulance crew, they seemed to accept the assessment that nobody had committed any obvious crime. Keith appeared, which strangely relieved some pressure. Having an adult family member present helped smooth things over, though there would be questions surrounding their mother and, as with any death within a home, an inquest would follow.

With Keith busy talking to the police, Stuart set the kettle on to boil while Mary drew up a stool and pointed at the coffee jar.

'Milk, sugar?'

She nodded, then stood watching.

Stuart pulled two mugs and offered the one with the sugar to Mary. Once both sat on a stool each, she spoke.

'Thank you.'

'I did nothing.'

Mary's hand left her mug, and her warm hand gripped his. 'You did. You came right when I needed you. I had no right to expect that after the way I treated you.'

Stuart understood. Finally, after listening to Phil Riley offer some back story and then today, seeing Mary's mother for the first time, the pieces fell into place. He had no right to judge her after everything she'd gone through.

He shielded her when they brought her father's body down and laid him on a trolley to take to the morgue. No matter what she thought of him, she didn't need to see that. Outside, he could hear the police medics along with Keith discussing plans. And then the ambulance drove away. No speeding through the lanes this time. There was no need.

Keith wandered in and headed straight to the sink, where he poured a tall glass of water. Even though he had his back to them, both Stuart could see Mary's body stiffen. This was one part of the family story which Phil Riley hadn't shared. Keeping one arm across Mary's shoulders, Stuart he let his eyes bore into Keith's back as though some hidden super power would vanquish whatever troubled Mary. The hulking figure turned and set his glass down.

'Well, sis. We can't say we're surprised. Stupid old man should have keeled over years ago.'

Mary's body trembled while Stuart looked on.

'So who's this then, your boyfriend?'

There didn't seem to be any malice in the question, though Stuart couldn't be certain. Seeing Mary's discomfort, he spoke for her.

'Just a friend. That's all. How are you? I know what you just said, but it still must be a shock.'

'Nah. It's like I said. Duffer had it coming.'

'Did they say what will happen now?'

Keith shrugged. 'I reckon they'll send over some busybodies to check on us all. For now, they seemed happy with the care I've been giving to mum. I guess we'll wait and see.'

Mary exploded. 'How dare you say that? You slacking bastard. I've done everything in this sodding house for years while you laze about and throw abuse.'

One hand shot up and for a second, Stuart thought she would throw a punch. Keith ducked backward.

'Hey, easy girl. We've both had some bad news. No need to get all hissy with me. We're family and need to stick together.'

Mary sat back and turned her head away while Stuart looked on bewildered.

'Are you going to help, then?' Stuart challenged. This wasn't his home or family, so the question held dangers, but Keith merely grinned.

'You're a cheeky shit, aren't you? Sure, why not. About time there were some improvements around here. I reckon Judith would like it here. It's about time I showed her my pad.'

'Who's Judith?' Mary queried sharply.

'Jesus, keep up, girl. Who'd you think I've been seeing all these months? Christ, I don't exactly like hanging around here with you moping on all the time and as for ma, well she ain't going to form a welcoming committee, is she?'

With that, Keith walked out of the kitchen.

Stuart remained for a further hour until Mary insisted they would be alright and he should go. They didn't kiss goodbye. Somehow, it didn't feel appropriate. He was determined to look out for her, though. If Keith gave her a hard time, he would not stand for it.

Chapter Twenty One

June 1983

DALEY'S PLANS WITH UNA weren't going the way he hoped. On their date, she'd been a swinging pendulum between scatty and downright horny. But now, she'd shelved her flirty behaviour in favour of clinging to him like a rat on a sinking ship. He felt distaste as he wondered how to escape her clutches. Somehow, whatever moves he made around the school, she seemed to know, popping up at the most inopportune moments.

Damn, he sulked. For a while he considered whether to contact the governors himself, though he barely knew them. Another thing which he should have pre-empted. Next, he wondered if he could approach Simmons, but dismissed the notion as quickly as it appeared. No, he would not help his rival. He needed something which would bring them both down.

The bell sounded and a group of sulky third years stumbled through the door in an uncoordinated display of unhappy mediocrity. Daley sighed again, though knew this offered an opportunity. Setting everyone to copy a chapter from their textbook, he stepped outside, knowing the kids would behave rather than suffer his wrath, and the school secretary would be back at her desk, assuming he'd be teaching. The corridors were silent as he carefully headed to the carpentry workshop and from there out to the deserted car park.

There were only around twenty cars and he immediately spotted Simmons' vulgar Rover sitting at one end of the row. Checking about him, Daley dashed across and crouched down. He felt nervous. A small sweat formed. Wiping across one sleeve, he extracted the Stanley knife taken seconds earlier from the woodwork store. After one last look, he drew the blade across one tyre and held it there until the hiss ended. Keeping low, he repeated the process until he'd slashed all four tyres. Satisfied, he cut a sliver of rubber he'd need later. He allowed himself only a few seconds before gathering himself and sprinting back to the main block, where he immediately dashed into the nearest toilet. After a brief inspection under the stalls, he grabbed several paper towels. Some were used to wipe his prints off, while the rest wrapped his precious parcel up to hide it away from prying eyes. Once covered and secured in his jacket, he relaxed and returned to the classroom. There remained one more part to his plan, but for now, he needed to maintain the pretence of teaching and establishing the pupils as his alibi.

If the mountain won't go to Mohammed, Daley thought as he shooed the children out of his class for lunch break. He headed straight for the downstairs offices. On the ground floor, a small hall buzzed with eager pupils all shuffling forward, keen to have some of the daily slop thrown onto their plates. Daley couldn't understand their vigour with the school canteen. He waited until his impatience got the better of him and he barged through the throng. The knife secreted in his pocket felt heavy as the boys buffeted into him, but he held his temper. Daley couldn't afford a scene while carrying the tool. Gripping the door handle, he wiped his forehead one more time and then marched in. The sight which met him, thrilled. Una's chair sat empty. Before anyone could enter, he unsheathed the knife and set it on the floor. Pulling the bottom drawer open, his eyes lit up. *Perfect.* Her handbag sat invitingly. Daley feverishly pulled at the clasp, and once open, he placed the blade inside the bag, making sure he tucked the extra sliver of black rubber in too. Then he placed everything back and stepped away to check the door to the hall. The crowds had barely thinned, which suited him as he slipped out and went to lunch.

Now all he had to do was conjure up a way to leak the location of the tool. Although he still had Simmons to deal with, Daley felt one weight lifted.

Mid afternoon came without incident and when the bell sounded for the last break of the afternoon, Daley strode out across the playground with purpose. He soon spotted the person he hoped to meet. Arthur Morgan had been the school caretaker as long as Daley could remember.

The aged custodian looked troubled.

'Are you alright, Arthur? You seem a bit flustered.'

'Too right I'm flustered, Mr Daley. I've just come up from the car park and someone has cut up Simmons' car, good.'

Daley feigned surprise.

'What? You mean some sods vandalised his car? When? What happened?'

'No idea when, but all four tyres are in tatters.'

'Bloody hell. Do you think someone from here carried out the attack?'

Morgan considered the theory.

'You know. It could just be. I locked all the gates apart from the main entrance once everyone had arrived for assembly and I have seen no visitors.'

'Shit. That will devastate him. He loves that car. Who do you think did it? I mean, Christ, they could be here right now somewhere. Do you think it's the kids?'

'Could be. There are enough of the little shits, though I can't say for sure.'

'Well, if they didn't, then that only leaves staff.'

'Surely not.'

'I agree, unlikely, but there is one person you need to tell about this and that's Simmons. Why don't you ask him who his enemies are and then let him call the police and point his finger.

Daley paced the classroom, waiting for news. His pupils were unusually quiet as they sensed his anxiety. He dismissed them seconds before the bell sounded, keen to discover Simmons' reaction. After chivvying everyone out of the room, he stormed off towards the offices. Before he'd even stepped halfway along the corridor, he skidded to a halt. Outside, he could see a police car heading for the school.

Swallowing hard, he pondered how best to play the situation. It took all his willpower to hold back and let things play out, but he stood firm, choosing to lurk close by.

He didn't have long to wait. Most of the students had rushed off home, though a few stragglers sensed gossip when the police arrived, but kept a sensible distance away. Daley moved towards the ground-floor hall. Despite keeping to the shadows, an agitated Simmons spotted him.

'Ah, Mr Daley. Glad you've appeared. Could you help round up all the staff for me? I need everyone in the school hall in five minutes.'

'Of course, Mr Simmons. Is anyone else already gathering them up?'

'Yes, Mr Morgan is covering the gymnasium and music room and Mr Knowles is covering the ground floor classrooms and the workshops.'

'Of course. I'll check the staff room and upstairs. I'll be back in a few minutes.'

As promised, Daley scooped up more members of staff, returning with him in the lead. A tense atmosphere greeted them as most teaching and support staff stood in uncertain clusters. Una Tavistock stood on the perimeter, isolated. In her arms, she held her handbag. Daley brushed one hand across his mouth to hide a wolfish grin.

A low level hum of conversation reverberated around the hall, though this ceased immediately when two uniformed police officers stepped through the door, followed by Simmons.

The head examined the group and, once everyone quietened down, he spoke.

'There's been an incident at the school today. An awful act of vandalism.' He gestured to the two officers. 'As you can see, I've summoned the police and they will require statements. I'm sorry to hold you all back this evening, but it is imperative we find the culprit and some of you may have seen something critical.'

Daley felt his body stiffen. He could see all his colleagues do the same.

'Thank you, head. If I may, I'll take things from here.' The voice came from the shorter of the two men in uniform. His stocky build and tone of voice conveyed a tough character who wouldn't stand any nonsense. 'As the head showed, we are here to cover the investigation into this crime. My name is Sergeant Pickering and with me is Constable Thorn and we are here to sort this out.'

A hand shot up. Daley saw Miss Rutt vying for attention.

'Yes?'

'Sorry. I... we were wondering, I know you said vandalism, but what happened? Did they damage any of our stuff?'

Daley looked away in disgust. The woman drove a revolting pea green Austin Princess, which stood as a carbuncle in the carpark. He wished he'd slashed those tyres, too.

In response to Rutt's questions, Simmons' head bobbed up and down. The action looked like a doll with a spring in its neck. Pickering was having none of it, and he raised a paw to quieten everybody back down.

'All in good time. Someone has committed a crime by slashing all the tyres on Mr Simmons' car. This appears a targeted attack and we are taking this extremely seriously.'

Daley's eyes narrowed as he scanned the room for reactions. As expected, most were aghast, though he detected mirth across a few faces and made a mental note of potential allies.

'Obviously, we need to start by identifying when this could have happened. For now, we are working on the likelihood that the perpetrator damaged the vehicle some time between 11 a.m. and 2 p.m. when Mr Morgan discovered the damage,' the sergeant continued.

'We will take statements from you all, but I'd like to start by asking if anyone has seen anything suspicious which could help us resolve this matter promptly. If you prefer, you can talk to either myself or PC Thorn privately, though, of course, if you have relevant information, it would be helpful if you shared it with us now.'

At the back of the group, a tentative hand rose. For most, the action went unnoticed, though Daley saw along with Simmons and the two officers.

'And you are?'

'Malcolm Osborne. I teach woodwork three days a week.'

Sergeant Pickering waved the man forward. 'What is it you think will be of use?'

The group of staff parted to leave Osborne a clear path to shuffle forward. His movement was painfully slow, and Pickering's face betrayed impatience.

'Thank you, sir. We appreciate your cooperation,' he said tersely. 'Now, you were saying.'

'It's just that one knife from the store is missing. I check the tools every day. I mean, you have to, with the toerags we have around here, but there's a gap in the rack, so someone must have lifted it.'

'When did you check these tools last?'

'I know the knife was there yesterday, but I didn't have any classes this morning, so I only saw after lunch.'

Osborne, along with PC Thorn, disappeared off to the woodwork stores. Once they had gone, Pickering asked all the staff to take a seat and once everyone settled, he chose the nearest teacher, Miss Rutt, to come to the front of the hall. From there, he directed her up onto the stage. Daley strained his ears, but it was no good. The sergeant and Daley's female colleague were just too far away.

Although restless, the group didn't have long to wait until PC Thorn, with Osborne scuttling along behind, came back into the hall. Thorn marched straight up to the stage, where he conversed with his superior.

'Could I have everyone's attention?' the sergeant barked. He held up a piece of metal, about six inches long. Daley was too far away to define the object clearly, but he knew exactly what it was. Pickering took the steps down and walked among the staff.

'This is an example of the missing knife. I'm not one for coincidences. So until we have a better explanation, I'd like to work on the theory that someone took one of these and then used it to slash Mr Simmons' tyres.'

The sergeant drew Simmons to one side, but returned seconds later.

'Mr Simmons and I have no desire to keep everyone here any longer than absolutely necessary, so here is what we propose. It is clearly too late to check every pupil's possessions as they've all gone home, so tonight we will conduct a bag search for everyone here and once we've cleared you, we will allow you to go. Unless, of course, you have anything critical to add this evening. Once we've completed that task, we will move on to check all the school lockers.'

The two police, with Simmons' help, pulled two tables over. The sergeant settled on one and the constable at the other.

Halleluiah, Daley thought.

Other staff protested.

'Come on Ned, we've nothing to worry about. We're just proving our innocence, after all.'

The group of staff thinned out as they reluctantly offered their bags and cases for inspection. Daley held back. Twelve staff ahead in the line stood Una Tavistock.

At last PC Thorn called her forward.

'Nothing to worry about, dear,' he said at seeing her nervous expression.

The constable popped the clasp on the handbag and looked inside. Immediately, his expression tightened, and he tipped the contents out. A metal object clattered out onto the table, closely followed by a black strip of rubber.

'Could you explain how you came to have this in your handbag?'

'But... that's not mine. I wouldn't. I mean, you can't possibly suggest I had anything to do with this,' she shrieked. Before the constable could react, Una Tavistock reached forward to grip the knife in order to scrutinise it. It would be a fatal error.

Everyone looked on in stunned silence until Pickering took charge. He stepped across, holding the knife, which they'd secured from the stores minutes earlier, while forcing Una to place hers back on the table. The two knives were identical. Next, he gripped the strip of rubber which he held aloft for her to see.

Turning to Ms Tavistock, the sergeant spoke gravely. 'I think you should accompany us to the station.'

Daley breathed out slowly, before turning his head slightly to one side. Inside he was shaking, though standing near the back of the line helped to mask his emotions. This had gone better than he'd hoped as he realised Una had unwittingly offered her fingerprints, which would compound her guilt.

Stunned silence reverberated around the hall, only broken by a solitary whimper as they took the school secretary away.

Chapter Twenty Two

When he wasn't at school or working on deliveries, Stuart gave all his time to Mary and the farm. At first, Keith balked at his repeated incursions, but soon he gave way and returned to his former behaviour, visiting the mysterious Judith. That suited both Stuart and Mary.

They'd sorted through her dad's belongings and found a dusty file, which contained a life policy. They didn't know how long it would take for the policy to pay out, or even where the money would go, but it seemed some good came of his death. But, as the only capable adult, Keith had to manage their income. Mary didn't seem to mind; she seemed to have a fresh spring in her step.

Today could be harder than before. The previous day, they'd laid Graham Fortune to rest. Stuart hadn't attended, and he wasn't sure what mood he'd find Mary. Arriving at the farm, he knocked. Stuart still didn't feel right about just barging in, despite Mary's encouragement. A high-pitched squeal prompted him to turn the handle and walk in.

'Cripes. I mean, wow. You look amazing.'

Mary stood, her face a radiant glow of colours. Her smile filled the room. She had transformed her hair into a luscious volume of colour and curls.

'Do you mean it? I mean, I'm not very good with this stuff, but I couldn't before... you know.'

Stuart went in and put his arms around her, kissing her.

'Sorry. I'm smudging your make up. Yes, I mean it. You're stunning. I love it. I just thought about yesterday. You know...'

Mary melted into his arms and lifted her mouth hungrily for another kiss. Clearly, the funeral wasn't about to be discussed.

'Wow, you are such a good kisser,' Stuart beamed. His mind buzzed with excitement, and it took all his willpower to remain composed. He didn't want to scare her, especially after her father's funeral. Reluctantly, he pulled away.

'Do you mean it?'

'Of course. I always thought you were beautiful. This make-up takes it to another level.'

She squeezed his hand. 'Good, 'cause once you moved away from Paul and the others, I worked out who you were, really.'

Stuart felt a guilty pang. He hadn't kept his promise to visit Paul a second time, and he forgot. His frown must have shown.

'What's up?'

'You didn't hear then?'

Mary's face pinched. 'Hear what?'

'Paul tried to kill himself.'

'You're joking. I... did not know. When?'

Stuart counted out the weeks on one hand. 'Early May,' he replied. *Shit, had it really been that long*? 'Yeah, he drank a load of shit and popped every pill in the house down his throat. He was really lucky his mum found him and called for help.'

'I don't like him, especially the way he used to look at me on the school bus, but it's sad this happened. I guess we don't always know what's really going on in others, do we?'

'I certainly didn't understand your life, and while I'm sad you lost your dad, I'm kind of relieved, too. I mean, if something hadn't changed, then I probably wouldn't be standing here right now. It's kind of you, what you just said about Paul.'

'It's not healthy to hold grudges.'

'Glad you agree. I went and visited Paul last month. He looked in a real crappy state, laid out on the hospital bed. You mentioning his name just now triggered. I don't think he has anyone in his corner these days, and I've broken a promise. I said I would go back and see him.'

'You should if it's important to you.'

Stuart marvelled at her kind comment.

'Blimey girl, you're one hell of a catch.'

'So, you've caught me, have you?'

Stuart hesitated. 'I mean, er... I'd really like to go out with you, but no, I don't want to catch you. I want you along with me, equal partnership.'

Her eyes twinkled, and he thought he detected a trace of mischief as she kept him waiting for a reply.

'You, sir, are my knight in shining armour and I would love to be your girlfriend. But before you get too comfortable, I want you to go see Paul. We agree, he has a history and in the past he's made me uncomfortable, but he's obviously got some problems. I think you choosing to stand by him is such a good thing to do.' She paused wistfully. 'Now I come to think of it. I can't remember when I last saw him go to school. Well, it's Sunday, so I think you should see how he is, otherwise we will have another week at school, and it'll be a struggle to find the time, especially as I'd like you back here for tea tomorrow.'

The gate creaked as Stuart entered the garden of the Winters household. It felt strange. He couldn't remember the last time he'd visited. Fear tugged at him. Would Paul's parents recognise him? Would they view him with distrust and tell him to pack his bags?

His finger hovered over the doorbell as he fought the urge to turn away. Mary's voice echoed in his head. The chime sounded and moments later, Sally Winters opened the door. Stuart stepped back. He felt his cheeks redden as he looked at the shrunken woman before him. His mouth felt dry, though he somehow managed a garbled noise which sounded a bit like 'Paul.'

'Hi, Stuart, nice of you to visit Paul. Come in. He's upstairs. He doesn't come down much these days. It's the first door at the top. Ask him if he wants a drink, will you? I'll get you one at the same time. Squash okay?'

Stuart nodded before climbing the stairs. Someone had painted the first door an ugly shade of grey. Not for the first time, he wondered just how little he knew about Paul. The fear returned as he prepared to knock. He quickly quashed those thoughts and rapped a knuckle against the wood. No sound came, so he tried again and this time, knowing Paul's mum had directed him to the correct bedroom, he turned the handle. Gloom filled the space. Stuart was sure he could detect a shape laid under the duvet. Taking Mary's kind words, Stuart stepped across the threshold and pulled open the curtains.

'Ma, leave me alone will you.'

'It's not your ma. It's Stuart. Though she asked me to see if you wanted anything to drink. She's lost a lot of weight since I saw her last.'

The covers shifted and a dark tatty head appeared before disappearing back under.

'You shouldn't be here. Nobody should.'

'I know, but I wanted to say sorry.'

Half a head poked back out.

'What have you got to apologise for? It's me who fucked everything up.'

'I promised I'd visit sooner, and I didn't. I should have, and I was wrong. Sorry.'

'I wouldn't worry about it. No other bastard cares. I wish they hadn't revived me.'

'You're wrong. I'm here. I felt bad I hadn't come before and that made me want to stay away, but I came and I'm here now. It's not much, but this mess your head is in. Whatever your brain is telling you, that you're alone, or that you are worthless, it's wrong. I'm here now.'

Paul's head sunk back under the cover and Stuart could see this would not be easy. He felt ill-equipped and almost hopped on one leg as he wavered. He stayed in limbo, pondering what to do.

A timid voice from below hooked his attention away.

'Here you go. I brought two beakers. One orange and one lemon. Paul likes both, so you can choose which you prefer.' With that, Paul's mother stepped away.

Stuart took it as a sign to stay. He took the glasses and placed the orange on a small table beside the bed. Now that he'd drawn the curtain back a little, he spied a small beanbag, so he settled himself, mirroring a pose of a gnome upon a toadstool. Taking tentative sips of the lemon, he waited. It was early afternoon, so wouldn't matter if he stayed until tea time.

Even though the pair didn't speak, a layer of calm settled. Stuart couldn't be sure, but he hoped this would be the beginning of Paul's recovery.

Chapter Twenty Three

ROGER DALEY'S EUPHORY AT the success of his plan to frame Una Tavistock quickly vanished after the weekend. He always found Mondays a drag and today was worse than usual. Simmons had tasked him with the registration of two classes. Ordinarily he'd just take care of the latest intake of first years in his role as form tutor, but today he'd have to look out for the third years as well. Apparently, Mr Thorpe was malingering under the guise of a man with the flu, though Daley didn't believe it.

Once he'd taken the register for his own class, he settled them down with some maths questions and then strode along the corridor. A chaotic sight greeted him, though everyone settled as soon as his wrinkled face peered through the door. He marched to the front desk, keen to get the tedious additional admin over with. Looking down the list, he recognised most and immediately started barking out names. Monotone voices sounded as each child responded, allowing Daley to place a tick against their moniker.

'Winters?'

Silence. Daley scanned the room; he couldn't see the lad.

'Has anyone seen Winters?'

'Off sick, sir,' a boy chanted.

Daley grunted in disgust. Slacking off, no doubt. Still, he felt troubled by the absence. Looking down, his brow furrowed at seeing a long line of crosses which stretched back for weeks. He hadn't known; he hadn't even noticed, and for the life of him, he couldn't recollect when he'd last seen Paul Winters.

Daley finished taking the register and returned to the other class, though his worrisome thoughts refused to go away.

Simmons sat behind his desk, rubbing his belly. His usual pains remained, though today he felt a weird elation. Genuine surprise tempered the feeling. His mouth had fallen open in shock when the police had searched Una's bag. He didn't believe she'd have the temerity to slash his tyres, but the evidence appeared damning. What a stupid fool, he considered, for keeping the knife upon her person; she deserved everything coming her way.

He'd detected some wavering when he'd spoken with the chair of governors just a couple of days earlier. On the surface, the chair had offered some agreement when he spoke about replacing the woman, though he felt sure the comments fed back were really empty platitudes. Not that it mattered now. Everyone had seen her shameful exit and there was no way she could come back. The thought gave him pleasure, and, for a second, he considered a celebratory drink. A stabbing pain in his side reminded him that not everything was well.

Simmons chose instead to check out the outer office, where he found a desk in a state of disarray. Sitting upon the normally pristine work area lay piles of registers and other administrative paperwork. Outside in the hall, noises came and went, but nobody came in and he doubted they would. He realised staff mostly stopped by to see the secretary. Bile formed at the back of his throat. Why'd they prefer her to him? His colleagues had treated him fairly before his promotion. Was it because he ran everything now?

After rummaging for some time, he found a phone directory; in it, a number for the agency. They didn't have anyone available for two days, but then at least he'd have some help to clear the backlog. As the receiver dropped back into its cradle with a gentle ding, he wondered what to do next.

Would Una have been his blackmailer? He pondered about it, but the idea seemed ludicrous. He supposed he couldn't rule her out. As before, his mind returned to the delivery of the first note. He wrestled with the fading memory. Had it been a boy heading off away from his front door, cloaked in a jacket and hood, or could it have been her? Damn, if only he'd opened the letter quicker, if only he'd dashed to the street sooner. Then he'd know for sure. It could have been her, though. Maybe.

He tried to lift the dark mood, but couldn't think of anything positive. A tow truck had taken his car away, with the garage blithely ignoring his requests to return the vehicle promptly. As a result, he had driven his wife's Mini into school, which felt as comfortable as sitting in a box of spanners. That was the problem with being in charge. Some days, he just wanted to go back to basics and teach, even if it was to a room full of insolent shits. He was sure someone somewhere would laugh at him, saying he should be careful what he wished for. Before he'd taken the role as head, everything was so much simpler. There could be no going back. All he could see was a monotonous procession until retirement finally arrived.

Damn, he needed that drink.

Stuart felt tired. His school assignments kept piling up, along with his normal deliveries for Phil Riley and evening visits to see both Mary and Paul. He wondered whether he'd ever catch a break. It was worth it, though. Every time he thought about Mary, his tummy fluttered and he thought about her a lot.

The progress with Paul felt stagnant. He spoke with Mary about it. She understood, and Stuart added yet another wonderful item to his list of her amazing qualities. He guessed this was down to her relationship with her mother, though this was one topic they had not spoken about. Ignoring his history homework for the third time that week, Stuart set out back to the farm.

'Hi,' Mary called as Stuart set his bike under the kitchen window. While Annie Lennox sang about sweet dreams, he waved back and wandered in. After sharing a gentle kiss, she asked for his help, pointing upstairs. His throat gulped as his mind considered exciting possibilities. It must have shown.

'Not *that,*' she laughed. 'Come on, I need help to bring mum downstairs for a few hours.'

Somewhat embarrassed, he joined in the laughing as they walked the stairs. Together they manoeuvred Mary's mum across the landing. Mary's blossoming influence showed even there. He'd seen her mother several times now and slowly he'd become accustomed to her zombie-like state. Today, instead of her usual plain white linen dress, she wore a summer dress sprinkled with pretty flowers. Despite only the tiniest flickers of emotions, the pattern somehow breathed life into the woman.

Her mum took direction easily and walked wherever they pulled her. The stairs were the trickiest part, being too narrow for the three, so Stuart went first, making sure nobody could fall. Everyone made it down safely and from there, Mary directed them to the family lounge. She'd clearly planned this, as blankets and a footstool sat to one side. Soon, they had her mother comfortably settled. Next, Mary switched on the television. It was the first time Stuart had seen the screen on within the farm. The programme looked grainy; she put on an episode of *All creatures great and small.*

With sunlight pouring through the window, Stuart examined Mary's mother.

'What happened to her? You know, to make her how she is?' He thought he knew the answer from Phil Riley, but he didn't want to let on Phil had told him.

'Someone attacked her. I don't know all the details, really. It happened before I was born.'

Stuart noticed her mother's head was misshapen. One side had an unnatural dent, and he winced as he considered the battering she'd received.

'Did they ever catch her attacker?'

Mary's face looked sad. 'No. And they won't. From what I've been told, there were no witnesses. It happened in the winter and they left her in the snow. It was a miracle someone found her.'

'I'm sorry.'

'Not your fault. You weren't even born back then.'

'So, when did it happen?'

'1967.'

Stuart did the maths.

'But that means... that means her rapist got her pregnant! Oh, I'm sorry Mary, that came out all wrong,' he said in anguish.

Mary blinked away a tear and nodded. Stuart's brain flipped as he tried to comprehend everything the poor woman must have gone through. Having her head smashed in like that. Rape and then being pregnant. He couldn't get his head around it.

'Are you okay talking about this?'

'It's difficult, but yes I am. I've never spoken to anyone about all this before and it helps. You've met Keith, he's not exactly Mr Sensitive and as for my dad,' she winced, 'well, he never sobered up to offer an opinion either way.'

'Was he always like that, you know, off his head on booze? Sorry, that wasn't clever of me.'

'It wasn't, but you're right.' Taking a deep breath, Mary continued, 'As you now know, Graham wasn't my real dad.'

He could see tears forming, which frightened and melted his heart in equal measure. This time, he rallied and stepped forward to hold her hand.

'Graham came along just after. He must have been amazing in the beginning, taking care of mum when she was pregnant, raising a child that wasn't his own.'

'I guess afterwards, everything got too much. It feels like I've been running the farm ever since I could walk.'

'My god. No wonder you withdrew all that time. I'm sorry. I really am. I just didn't know.'

'It's done. It happened, and it shaped me. You've nothing to apologise for. In fact, you are my little hero.'

'Hey, less of the little.'

Another thought pinged across Stuart's brain.

'So Keith is not your brother?'

'No, he's Graham's son. I think he resents me coming along with my mum in tow, like some kind of leech. I can't blame him really.I mean, what kind of stepmother did he get? And I know you've only seen Graham as a drunk, but there he was, stepping in to marry and care for a pregnant woman who spent every day practically in a coma. I know it didn't take long for the whole facade to crumble. But he started out with the right intensions.'

'I guess. It's difficult, as I've only known the bad times, but thank you for sharing that. Maybe there is good in everyone.'

'Maybe. Though I'm not sure I'd say the same about my mum's attacker. Whoever it is, he's evil, and she deserves justice.'

Chapter Twenty Four

July 1983

HELP FINALLY ARRIVED IN the first week of July. The Fortune family would, at long last, receive visits from a care worker. There had been paperwork and lots of bluster from the council, but in the end, everything was sorted. As Keith had said he'd taken care of his mother, the council was reluctant at first but caved in after some visits of social services. They'd realised it was Mary who had taken care of her invalid mother, as they stated in their report. Mary bridled at the term. Her mother wasn't someone of lesser worth. She needed help, that's all.

The woman, called Fatima, came as a breath of fresh air. Twice a week she'd call in and attend to Mary's mother's personal care and any jobs needed around the house. For the first time in her life, Mary had the freedom to roam without guilt. Often she spent time with Stuart, but sensing she'd neglected her friendship with Bobbie, she made a call.

'Hi. It's me. Yeah, I know. What were they thinking showing that on *Top of the Pops*?'

A giggle sounded at the opposite end of the line.

'Listen, I was thinking. You've never been to the farm before. Would you like to come over for tea?'

It sounded lame compared to the welcome Bobbie's household offered; she had little by comparison, but she wanted to show her her place.

'Love to. It's outside the village, isn't it?'

Mary relayed directions and arranged a time.

'Great. Since you have no neighbours close by, we can turn up the music.'

'Good. Make sure you bring a decent mix tape then.'

Paul's bedroom had become his cell. Stuart was the only visitor and he appreciated it. He still hadn't returned to school, would not until the start of the new year. That made everything harder.

Nobody else cared. Harry, Eddie and Bruno hadn't bothered to contact him, and he knew they wouldn't. Empathy wasn't high on their agenda and he couldn't cope with their ridicule. He hadn't heard from Daley either, which confirmed his fear their fling or whatever they had was over. It left him feeling confused. He didn't understand why Stuart continued to stick by him and from what he'd heard, Mary seemed to be in his corner, too. Guilt weighed as he considered how he'd treated them both.

It would take time and he wasn't ready to leave his home, but things felt like they were levelling off at least, he thought hopefully before his face fell. Who was he kidding? He liked boys. No one would understand, not even Stuart and Mary.

He cried his heart out. The only one who understood him was Daley, his betrayer. Paul's whole body rocked as his sobs intensified.

One downside of getting rid of Una was the lack of information. The old crone had gushed gossip like a fountain. The temporary replacement knew nothing, well, nothing of value to Daley at least.

'Good morning, Mr Simmons,' Daley offered before walking away, not in the mood for talking. Damn, even the head seemed to be cheerful today. Once he rounded a corner at the end of the corridor, Daley leaned against the wall. Was that it? Had he finally given up on his ideals to have the odious fool removed from the job? The trouble was, he knew he could be a suspect if he tried sending threatening notes again. There *had* to be a better way.

He also couldn't stop thinking about Paul. Why had he been absent for so many weeks? What was going on? There was no way he could ask about him. People would be suspicious, as Paul was in a different year now.

He felt thoroughly fed up and frustrated. He had few allies within the teaching and support staff and even fewer within the governors. Unless he could figure a way to prove Simmons as incompetent, he knew any chance of his own progression would fail. He had to come up with something, and it would need to be spectacular.

'Wow, so this is your farm. It's amazing, look at that view!'

'Come on, Bobbie. There's someone you need to meet.'

Tugging her friend's arm, Mary pulled Bobbie into the farmhouse. Ahead, a program sounded out from the television, but before they could enter the room, Mary drew to a halt.

'Prepare yourself. This may be a little shocking for you. My family isn't quite like yours.'

Her friend frowned in confusion, so, taking a deep breath, Mary led her into the lounge.

'Bobbie, I'd like you to meet my mother.'

'Hi, Mrs Fortune. Erm, what's wrong with her?'

'She's been like this all my life. Kinda shaped me, really. You get now why I was so closed off when we first met.'

Bobbie just shook her head.

'Yes, of course. Oh Mary, I wish I'd known.'

'I should have said, but really, put yourself in my shoes. It's not an easy topic to throw into the conversation. What should I have said, "Hi my name's Mary and my mum is practically a zombie"?'

'Yes, I see. Does she know we're in here?'

'I think so, but it's weird. I've never heard my mother speak; some days I think I see a spark, though it always vanishes just as fast.'

'Christ, and I complain when my family won't shut up. Well, you've got me here now and if your mum doesn't mind, we should play some tunes.'

'She won't mind and if you can get her up and dancing, I'd be the happiest girl.'

'You seem brighter lately. I know being around me will do that, but anything else?' she grinned.

'Yes, I am happy,' Mary declared, a glint in her eyes.

'Go on,' Bobbie prompted.

'I've got a boyfriend now.'

'No way! You're a dark horse. Come on, spill.'

Mary blushed as she told Bobbie all about Stuart.

Bobbie hugged her. 'I'm so happy for you. He sounds interesting, though I don't want him interfering with our moves...'

'He won't, he's lovely, though I haven't seen him dance,' Mary giggled. 'Come on. Which mix tape did you bring?'

Bobbie dipped into her bag and brought out a selection, which she scattered on the carpet.

Mary scanned the choices. 'I know we've heard it a hundred times, but let's start with Culture Club.'

Placing the tape into the machine, she pressed play before turning up the volume. The music drowned out the television on the opposite side of the room, but no one complained.

Stuart chuckled as he rode towards the farm. Even though the building was still a way off, he could hear music. He marvelled at Mary's transformation. She's really come out of her shell, he thought. It hadn't been so long since he'd lurked and watched in silence. As he opened the side door and through the kitchen, he could make out a pair of voices singing.

He frowned, not sure what was going on. The music played loudly and as he peered through the doorway, he could see Mary's mother. As usual, her vacant expression offered no clues to whatever was happening. As he nudged forward, he saw Mary pirouetting holding a hairbrush as a makeshift microphone. She waved as he approached, and then Stuart noticed the other girl, mirroring Mary's moves. Whoever she was, she had her eyes closed so hadn't detected his presence. He stepped forward and gave Mary a peck on the cheek before diving back away from the other girl's flailing arms.

Mary grinned and turned the volume down.

'Hey, what? Oh, hi.'

'Hi. I'm Stuart, you must be the famous Bobbie.'

'So, you've heard of me then,' she winked.

'Mary thinks you're fab. Love the singing and your moves, by the way.'

The two girls pouted.

'Music was loud, though. I could hear you all the way down the lane.' He looked across. 'Not enough to get a reaction though, I see.'

Stuart kicked himself inwardly as he detected Mary's head dropping. 'Come on. Let's see if the three of us dancing in front of her could make a difference.'

The smile returned and seconds later, with the volume cranked up to the max, the three teens started belting out the lyrics to "Total eclipse of the heart."

Chapter Twenty Five

August 1983

WITH HELP FROM FATIMA, Mary moved her mother down to the lounge, where they set the television playing. The visits from the care assistant were proving really useful. They'd already discussed changing the layout of the dining room to covert the area into a ground floor bedroom.

Stuart's help had been welcome as they moved the furniture around. The hardest job had been to remove the dining table and chairs. Now, with the clearing job complete, Mary was contemplating colours.

'What shall we go for?'

'I don't know. What was her favourite colour?' Stuart asked before realising his mistake. 'Sorry. I guess you don't know. What about you? Which colour do you like the most?'

'It's got to be something bright for me, though I don't just want one colour. Maybe yellow across that wall and some blue over there. I picture a field of sunflowers beneath a beautiful cobalt sky.'

'I love it,' he said, hugging her. 'I'll try to nag my dad to drive us somewhere to buy what we need.'

'Oh, my hero,' she joked.

While Stuart tried to work out how much paint they'd need, Mary stepped next door to pour a drink.

'You want some?'

'No thanks, but your mum may be thirsty.'

She drew down two beakers and filled them both, adding a glug of squash into her own. After setting hers on the side, she moved towards the lounge.

'Hi, Mum,' she called. As usual, her mother was staring impassively at the television screen. Placing her drink safely on the side, Mary knelt down, took her mother's hand and looked into her face. She knew her mother wouldn't recognise her. Despite this, she gave her a gentle squeeze.

As Mary got up, the film's ending credits played out. A haunting tune of twangs, whistles, and cries. With no warning, out of the blue, her mother lifted one arm and pointed.

Mary wept into Stuart's shoulder. She couldn't believe it. If she hadn't witnessed it with her own eyes... Fatima came in the room, but the pointing finger had dropped and everything returned to normal.

'What just happened?'

'I... don't know. I placed her drink down, held her hand and said her name, and then she just pointed. You saw it.'

Mary repeated the process over and over. No matter what she did, there was no reaction.

'Mum! Come on, Mum. You're in there. I know it. You just showed me.'

Fatima put a hand on Mary's shoulder. 'It's okay, she's there. Don't make her agitated. Where did your mother point?'

Mary calmed down. She wasn't sure. It had to be somewhere across the room. 'There. The television, I think.'

'Makes sense. Okay, Mary, think hard. What was playing when this happened?'

She couldn't fathom. Some kind of western film, but which one? Only the haunting tune remained. She tried humming the tune but gave up quickly, looking imploringly towards the others. A few seconds later, Stuart bolted out the door. She heard him shout he wouldn't be long, and within ten minutes, he'd returned waving a copy of that week's TV listings.

Mary snatched the copy and immediately started searching. There, 6:30 p.m. the news bulletin and listed right before, showed a film, *The Good, the Bad and the Ugly.*

At first Mary marvelled at Stuart's idea, but in the three days it had taken to locate a VHS copy, her doubts had overridden all hopes. He had been a star. Not only by bringing the video player to her house from his home, but he'd set the fiddly device up and had spent hours in Oxford looking for a copy of the film.

The television hissed as grey dots filled the screen while her mum sat, stationed as before. Mary couldn't bear the tension as Stuart loaded the cassette. A click sounded, followed by a whirr. Then came the trailers; Stuart forwarded on. At last, the movie started.

Nothing happened. Mary couldn't contain her disappointment. 'Come on, Mum,' she begged.

'Let's try this,' Stuart offered. He reached down to press the fast-forward button.

Three agonising minutes later, he set the film playing again. This time, the film was about to end.

The credits rolled, moving up the screen quicker than Mary would have liked, but still nothing. Mary wept, burying her head into Stuart's chest while he held her close.

'Wait. Look.'

It wasn't much, but there was movement. A solitary finger wavered, more at the carpet than anything, but Mary smiled happily through her tears. They'd made a connection.

Today would hopefully give some answers, Mary thought. They'd finally been able to make an appointment with a neurologist. Fatima had arranged a specially equipped minibus, and together the three of them would visit a neurologist at the hospital. It helped to have Fatima there. The woman oozed calm efficiency, and when their driver delivered them all to the John Radcliffe hospital, Mary looked on in awe as the woman swept inside the building, to return only seconds later with a wheelchair.

'There you go, Mum,' Mary said, once her mother sat in the chair. 'Is it okay if I push?'

Fatima smiled and nodded, before leading the way. They walked towards the neurologist's office, Doctor Slee. An assistant helped them and had explained that Mary's mother needed to undergo some tests.

Mary looked across at her mother's still form, rigged up to some sort of machine using wires which were taped to her forehead. The whole rig looked alien, and Mary wondered what they hoped to gain from the exercise. A mechanism whirred, spitting out a thin strip of paper which reeled outward until it touched the floor to settle in a delicate coil. All along the strip, meaningless lines wavered like some secret code.

Doctor Slee tried several tests while Mary looked on impatiently. Each time he scribbled on a chart.

As expected, her mother remained immobile.

Finally, the doctor spoke. 'I'm afraid I cannot tell you anything decisive yet. Please, understand there is so much we still don't understand about the human brain. Clearly, there are triggers as you have found, Mary, but the mind is a network of interconnecting pathways. When they become damaged, as with your mother's head trauma, doors get closed. I know this sounds bleak, but sometimes the brain can rebuild those pathways. Think of it like the road network. If you can't take the road from Oxford direct to Aylesbury, then they could just drive to Bicester and head across. The route may differ, though the end goal remains the same.'

Mary's voice cracked in frustration, 'You mean you cannot tell me *anything*?'

'No, not yet. I'd like to see you both again in one month,' he responded.

'What? That's it, you're sending us away? But you haven't helped her.'

'Hey. It's okay,' Fatima interjected while tugging gently on Mary's sleeve. 'Doctor Slee isn't abandoning either of you. He has to look at the test results he's just gathered and while we wait to come back, we have a programme of things we can try out. It won't be long and we will come back to move this forward more.'

Mary glared at her carer. Reluctantly, she accepted what Fatima said. 'Fine, but you'd better show me this plan of yours. Mum isn't getting any younger, you know.'

'Don't worry. I promise. Come on, let's get your mother home.'

After thanking the doctor, Mary wheeled her mother back out of the hospital and along to the minibus.

'Well, that was an anti-climax.'

'Be patient. As Doctor Slee said, there are so many things about the brain we just don't understand. We will get there and one day we'll get some improvement.'

Fatima checked her watch and had a few words with the driver.

'Great,' she said once everyone had buckled up. 'I've spoken with the driver and he's going on a quick detour before we head home.'

'Oh? Where are we off to?'

'Just somewhere pretty for a change of scene. You'll see.'

Craig Simmons sat on a bench overlooking Cutteslowe Park in Oxford, his favourite place. Closing his eyes, he inhaled deeply. The fresh air always settled him. Swarms of noisy children milled about, some kicking balls while others marvelled at the miniature railway, but he'd chosen to sit further away where the dappled shade kept him at just the right temperature. He looked about, though the children appeared too young to come from his school. That was a relief. He lacked both the empathy and patience to engage with his own students. After chastising himself for leaving his latest paperback at home, he closed his eyes in an attempted doze.

The first disruption came when the wind whipped up, forcing a tin can to blow along the path. It made a gentle clattering noise as it bounced, just enough for one eye to open.

Jesus, Simmons thought. He hated to see his pristine space sullied with litter. He couldn't spy a bin nearby and with the can heading further away, he returned to his daydream. It was rare for him to have pleasant thoughts these days, but today was an exception. He drew peaceful imagery from his surroundings.

Soon after, though, a second event broke his spell. This time, the disruption came from a slobbering hound. Distaste etched across Simmons' face as the dog offered a slime covered ball for him to throw. Its tail wagged furiously. Looking at Simmons with its huge brown eyes, the animal dropped the ball, tilting its head. Instinctively, fearing a bite, Simmons raised both knees in defence. The action offered no deterrent as a wet nose nudged forward. He could feel his tranquil mood evaporating as the dog persisted. Just as he contemplated lashing out with both feet, a shout sounded and a man ran over.

'Sorry about that. He's lovely, isn't he, but a little too affectionate. I'll take him out of the way.' The owner walked off, oblivious to any discomfort caused.

Simmons had planned on staying for another hour, but the repeated intrusions left him feeling unsettled. Annoyed, he stood and marched back towards his car. The walk wasn't far, though the sun beating down made him sweaty. He took off his jacket and contemplating walking along Port Meadow instead.

Once back at the car park, he fumbled with his keys. The driver's side door always stuck, further souring his mood. The lock resisted and despite knowing the mechanism would stick, he pushed the key harder, without success. His fruitless jabbing continued until, realising he risked snapping his key off in the lock, Simmons stepped back. Irritated, Simmons walked around to the passenger side to try the opposite door.

'Hi, Mr Simmons. Nice to see you here.'

Blinded by dazzling sunshine, Simmons' looked up uncertainly trying to identify who'd spoken.

As they closed the gap, he identified three people heading along the path. The girl was the one who'd spoken. Was she one of his pupils? He couldn't be sure. Alongside her stood an older black woman and then, casting his eyes downward, Simmons' stomach dropped. It *couldn't* be. Surely not. Not after all these years.

'Are you okay?'

Simmons froze. He was unable to speak. In the end, he mumbled something about needing to go and the trio continued on their way. It took him several minutes to unlock the passenger door, where he flopped inside. He could feel sweat pooling across the base of his spine as his whole body shook. The last time he'd seen the woman in the wheelchair had been almost seventeen years earlier on an icy winter's night. Despite glazed eyes and a disfigured forehead, he knew her.

Anyone passing by, should they care to look closely, they'd have seen a man rocking back and forth, with both arms wrapped across his torso.

'Did you see that?'

'What?' Fatima replied.

Mary drew her mother's wheelchair to a halt. 'Mr Simmons, back there.'

Fatima looked around, confused, before answering. 'Oh, you mean that guy back there? I guess he seemed odd rattling his car door like that. Why?'

'He's the head of our school. That's why I said hello, but that isn't what I meant. He looked fine when he saw both of us, but not when he looked at mum. I don't know what it was, but he looked as though he'd seen a ghost.'

'Now you come to mention it, he froze up. Probably just a summer cold or something. Come on, let's show your mother the park and see if we can't nurse some life back into her.'

Simmons couldn't go home. Not yet. Not after meeting Emily again after all those years. He wasn't sure how long he'd remained in his car, but eventually he gathered himself and forced his obese body over to the driver's seat. He couldn't face the possibility Emily and, he supposed, her daughter would head back to the car park. Feverishly, he jangled the keys to leave. It took a while, but once the car started, he stamped down on the accelerator, causing a cloud of dust as the car's new tyres bit into the dirt. Two near misses later, Simmons found his destination with a bump. The car park ahead stood empty, yet he'd still misjudged the entrance. Now a metal post leaned over in a mangled state, while his own bumper hung low enough to scrape along the road. He nursed his car into a space and parked. In front of him, the Oxford landmass known as Port Meadow appeared deserted. Leaving his car unlocked, he removed his jacket and set out to walk.

In front of him lay the River Thames; behind a bridge above the railway line. Both places offered the ultimate solution, Simmons thought, utterly confused. Until he could think properly, he opted for the middle of the meadow. A fresh breeze blew across the plain, offering the peace he'd hoped for earlier, only now he couldn't settle.

He would have brought her here. He knew that. Their relationship had been wrong, with him the teacher and her just a sixteen-year-old pupil. Not only that, back in 1966, Simmons had been engaged to Molly. She would never understand. How could she?

Simmons' head hurt as all the memories came back in a flood. The furtive meetings, hiding away from prying eyes while they kissed and more. *Oh, God,* he thought as vivid images returned. It wasn't his fault, he reconciled. He was merely guilty of weakness. Emily had been the one. She'd led him on with her inviting eyes and lips, her seductive body. He could still feel the burning desire; their kiss, full of promises, was burned into his memory. He felt himself harden and immediately he sank to the ground in a disgusted sob. Everything about the memory was wrong, yet he knew he would never feel elation like that again.

The hours passed. Nobody came, but with its daily inevitability, the sun sank lower into the sky and with it came the colder air. Molly would worry, despite the poor state of their marriage. Thinking about the deplorable state of their marriage worsened his mood. Placing his head in both hands, Simmons wondered where it had all gone wrong.

All he'd ever wanted was to be happy. For a brief while, his illicit affair with Emily had taken him to undiscovered heights, but that hadn't lasted. Simmons knew about the attack, of course, though he only learned about it a few days after. Those were some of his darkest days. Even now, he did not know how he'd kept everything from his future wife. Losing Emily tore him apart. He couldn't visit, not to the hospital or even when they brought the poor girl back to her farm in Ascot Midden. How could he explain his presence?

Slowly, things settled though people, including the police, asked questions. He'd been a wretch, and he knew it. Realising he faced scandal or possible imprisonment, Simmons allowed himself to fade from view. He knew if they dug deep enough, they'd find their trips to places like the cinema. For months he lived in fear, but the knock on the door never came and finally he found peace with Molly instead. Only now, his marriage rocked on an uneasy axis.

By the time he arrived back at the car park, the light had almost gone. In the dim gloom, he kicked the bumper, which snapped away with a loud clang. Reaching down, he gripped the driver's door handle and pulled. It opened, perhaps the only thing which had gone right all day.

Chapter Twenty Six

September 1983

PAUL LOOKED OUT FROM his bedroom as raindrops trickled down the windowpane. He could see Stuart approach, and he knew what was coming. Today, at least he'd bothered with dressing and climbing out of bed.

Scooping up the dirty laundry, he made room for his friend and then, he stepped out of his room to head downstairs.

'Coke?' he offered when his mum had brought Stuart through to the kitchen.

'Sure. It's good to see you up and about, especially on such a shit day. Here, can you hang my coat somewhere to dry?'

After taking care of the jacket and grabbing a couple of tins, Paul led the way upstairs. He was pleased about Stuart's visit, though their friendship still felt weird.

'I can't do it. I can't go in tomorrow,' he declared once the pair had settled in private.

'Course you can. It's just school. You're not a first year anymore. It'll be okay.'

'Easy for you to say. I've had months away.'

'That could be a good thing. Maybe it'll be like you're a new starter? Anyway, I know it's easy for me to say, but putting it off will only make things harder. Once you've done your first day back, we can hang out and talk it through. The school knows what happened, and it's their job to look out for you.'

Paul cringed as shameful thoughts pounced. It must have shown.

'Hey. There's no disgrace, you know. You had a bad time, but you're bouncing back.'

The kind words could not convince Paul. He knew just how badly people could behave. His lips pursed together.

'Are you still taking the tablets they gave you?'

Paul stared at a Duran Duran poster before replying.

'Yeah. I'm not as wobbly now.'

Later, when Stuart finally left, Paul stepped back into the kitchen to examine his anti-depressants. The jar rattled in his grasp, half full. The doctors had recommended his dosage and, after talking to his parents, everyone had agreed the pills would live downstairs. In the beginning, the system worked well, but within a few days, Paul knew the tablets weren't for him. Dizziness and headaches coupled with constant nausea all conspired to keep him awake each night. As the fatigue grew, he took direct action. Misleading his parents had been remarkably easy. Neither of his parents found watching him take the pills easy viewing. They'd wince and look away, so hiding them to flush away later, instead of swallowing, took no effort.

Paul sat in the middle of the bus, taking them to school. He'd seen Mary and there'd been a brief nod, but nothing more. As she looked away, Paul's mind turned inward in fear. Although he did not know what was to come, his brain had already started filling in the blanks. A deepening unease seeped through his being.

The bus stopped in the next village, and another girl appeared. He thought he recognised her. Whoever she was, she made a beeline for Mary, who happily removed her bag to offer a spare seat. Immediately, Paul could see they were friends. Would that help him at all?

The bus paused at a set of traffic lights half a mile from their destination. The red light appeared to pulse in Paul's vision, mirroring his heart, which now thundered within his chest. He had to get out. He couldn't do this. Turning his head, he stared forward, both hands gripping the headrest, knuckles white and shaking. Paul stood as confused thoughts moved towards desperation. The light changed to green, and the bus surged forward. The action jolted him back into his seat where he sat, holding his head in his hands.

When they arrived, Paul sat still. Even when other pupils buffeted his head as they clumped down the aisle, he didn't move.

'Oi. Come on, clear off. I can't take you to the depot, you know.'

The driver broke Paul's stupor; he stood and stumbled towards the exit. Outside, the air felt chilly. He leaned against the brickwork and watched as his breath blew out in a neat plume. He wished he could vanish like that, but the solid wall pinned him to the present. The cold helped to disguise the trembling he felt, and he observed, alone, the others disappear into the school. It wasn't by far Paul's first year at Chancery School, yet now he felt worse than when he'd arrived that first day. Most pupils had disappeared inside and, once again, Paul considered whether to walk away. What would it matter if he flunked out of school? While he dithered, he saw Mary. She'd almost reached the outer doors with her friend when she turned and muttered something. Quickly, she scuttled over.

'Hi Paul,' she said, looking nervous. 'You can't stay out here. It's freezing. Everything will be okay once we're inside.'

He nodded automatically, still unclear what he wanted to do. She gently tugged his arm and once he followed, she let go. Her invisible magnet kept his feet moving forward until both stepped inside and the door closed to shut off the outside world.

'Come on, otherwise we'll be late.'

Her pace quickened, and he moved off along the corridor. Ahead, the chatter of their classroom intensified. Mary walked in while Paul held back in the doorway. She glided through the crowd and he realised just how much she'd changed from the meek girl he once knew. His eyes narrowed as he took in the other pupils from the safety of the doorway shadow.

'Come on, dumbass. Don't stand there. Get your arse in here.'

The voice carried across the chatter, causing Paul to wither, and a raucous cheer erupted. In the furthest corner, Harry stood, wearing a huge grin while waving him in. He nudged forward, reluctant, yet somehow compelled. Paul scanned the room, desperate for allies. Eddie and Bruno sat in the same corner as Harry, though that merely compounded his fears. In the middle, closer to the front, sat Mary and her friend but no spare seats were available near them. In the end, he spied a desk at the front of the class. Head bowed slightly, he shuffled forward to take a seat.

Paul sat and waited, head staring forward, intensely focussing on the board and nothing else. Was this how a condemned prisoner felt at finally being confronted by a noose? Behind him, the furore continued, and Paul could feel the body shakes returning as he struggled to tune the noise out. He looked down, counting the fingers on each hand, one, two... ten, eleven, twelve. No, that couldn't be right. He tried again, slower. This time he only got as far as four before his noisy classmates forced him to shake his head and lose his place. Maybe, if he could just count the digits on one hand, he'd be alright. With agonizing slowness, he lifted his left fist and splayed his fingers. Holding his hand just centimetres away from his face, he tried again. Tears formed, obscuring his vision, compounding his frustration, and a wave of dizziness swept over him. He could feel his body slumping, yet felt powerless to prevent the slide. The noises sounded muddled now, distant. As he moved down towards the classroom floor, his brain seemed to suspend. Now the chatter seemed to ease. Yes, that felt better. His eyes flickered, though only a grey dirge of muddled images registered, and then his head hit the floor and everything turned to black.

'Sir. It's Winters. He collapsed in class. Come now.'

Daley turned, eyes wide, before he recovered his normal composure. He didn't recognise the messenger, but the wide eyes and tugging arm showed it wasn't a sick joke.

'Where is he now?'

The boy pointed a shaky hand and Daley sprinted off. Seconds later he arrived at the classroom. Everyone just stared, in silence. Shoving them out of the way, he saw Paul Winters' prone form.

'Get back, will you?' he barked. 'And someone call for an ambulance.'

A few moved cautiously backward; when nobody ventured out of the room, he screamed at the nearest to make the call.

'You, go with him,' he shouted, pointing at a second pupil. They vanished and Daley knelt down and cradled Paul's head. It felt warm and as he leaned in he could sense breathing, but the move stirred another more intimate memory.

'He's breathing. Everyone, stand outside in the corridor. Wait there in silence until help comes and send them in.'

While Daley took his jacket off to support Paul's head, the shocked students filed outside. Once alone, he cradled the boy's head while a flood of unexpected emotions filled his mind.

Mary shouted for Stuart. She thought he'd be working at the shop so had headed there as soon as the bus dropped her back from school.

'Hi Mary. What's up? Stuart won't be back for a while. I sent him off with some deliveries. Are you alright? You look a state.'

'Phil, it's awful. Something happened to Paul. He went into school with me today and...' she gathered herself. 'He had some kind of seizure. One minute he sat in front of us and the next he kind of slithered down to the floor.'

Mary leaned against the counter while Riley cupped an arm around her neck.

'That's terrible. I'm really sorry to hear this. That boy sure has gone through a tough time. Is he going to be alright?'

'I think so. I heard he's back home now and someone said about it being a panic attack.'

'He's going to need a bit of care from now on. Are the teachers doing anything?'

Mary considered this. 'Yes, I think so. Mr Daley normally gives us a hard time. On any other day, I'd call him creepy, but today he seemed to care.'

Chapter Twenty Seven

DALEY FELT UNNERVED, HIS usual stoic and controlled behaviour replaced by agony and sadness because of Paul's collapse. He'd unearthed most of the story regarding the overdose and he'd witnessed the panic attack. He felt powerless, seeing Paul in such a state, not able to do anything about it. There was no way he could get close to the boy, not like before. People would talk.

He was confused. Why would Paul have fallen apart? Surely everything between them had been amazing, yet clearly something had changed. As he paced the rooms in his flat, he considered what to do. He couldn't control Paul, but at least the boy had kept quiet about their secret.

And then there was Simmons. The bloated oafishness of the man caused Daley to seethe. Since the start of the new term, the head's behaviour had worsened. Once again, he dismissed the notion of more blackmail. This time, a new idea brewed. He'd need something shocking which would shake the school to its core in order to prove Simmons ineptitude. With an upcoming Halloween party, Daley thought he may just have found a way.

Progress with Mary's mother seemed inexplicably slow. However, there were signs and given how long she'd been in her state, she could bear a few more months. They had a new routine at least, which showed promise. Now they'd moved her mum's bedroom downstairs, things were a little easier. Every day, often with either Fatima or Stuart present, they would play parts of the video. Some days, they had no reaction. Those were the long days, when Mary felt everything slip back, but sometimes the opposite happened. She'd even seen what looked like a controlled blink, which had caused her heart to race with joy. The hand gestures had repeated too, though the pointing finger always looked feeble.

What really burned was the lack of communication. Her mother clearly looked happier and showed signs of improvement, but so far, she had not uttered one word. Despite all Mary's endeavours, they were far away from any kind of dialogue.

Both Fatima and Doctor Slee had offered reserved encouragement, though there were only so many times Mary could bear them say it would take time. Stuart and Bobbie had also been amazing. Mary still couldn't get over the freedom she now had since her dad had passed; Stuart had become a daily visitor and Bobbie came to the farm almost as often. With Fatima helping with her mum, everything had become a lot easier, especially since she'd organised visits to a day centre. For the first time in years, Mary arrived at school every day.

One person remained absent, Paul. Mary knew Stuart kept in touch, but it had been a while since she'd heard any news. Today, though, Mary returned to Chancery's, keen to resume her lessons.

Once she'd stepped off the bus, her eyes searched for Bobbie. Normally she'd see her friend underneath the weeping willow which sat alongside the playing fields, but not today. Today, Harry and his thug cronies, Bruno and Eddie, occupied the spot. She withdrew with distaste on her lips. The bullies' tenure remained a problem within the school. She turned to head inside.

'Hey, there you are,' Bobbie chimed enthusiastically. 'I wondered if the bus had dropped you off. Look at this.'

Mary allowed her friend to pull her along until they stood outside the music room. She cast a lacklustre glance at the noticeboard. Bobbie offered an animated gesture.

'Look!.'

On the surface, the poster looked bland and uninspiring, as though someone had used a highlighter pen, barely trying. The message was simple: the school would have a Halloween dance, scheduled for Saturday 29 October. She could see Bobbie getting impatient, but Mary hadn't finished reading.

'What do you think?' Bobbie asked while bouncing up and down like an animated rabbit.

Mary wasn't sure. Bobbie had recently taken a shine to Sting. The two of them duetting "Every breath you take" in her bedroom was one thing, in front of all the other pupils in a crowded school hall quite another. She needed time to think about it, but Bobbie clearly wanted an answer.

'I don't know. What if Harry and his cronies turn up?'

'What if they do? There will be hundreds of us here and the teachers, plus you know the best bit.'

Mary looked confused.

'Oh, come on Mary. We will have make-up. Just picture it. Sure, everyone will dress up as monsters, but I can't wait. Say you'll come, please. It won't be the same without you.'

Mary caved. Despite her reservations, she had to admit the dressing up did sound like fun.

Stuart wasn't too enthusiastic about the dance, his first thought her safety. But now Mary had made a promise to Bobbie, she intended to keep it.

Mollified that the girls would be together, at least, he wondered what else he could do to protect her. That was when the idea came to him.

'Look, it will work. I mean, how will they know?'

'Are you nuts? Do you seriously want to bump into Simmons, or Daley?'

'Of course not, but it won't happen. It will be dark, and loud and everyone will be in fancy dress. All we need is a monster mask, and I can sneak in with everyone else. There's no way the teachers can police a dance that size.'

'I guess. It would be lovely to sneak somewhere dark for a kiss.' Stuart could think of several places where they could manage a cuddle in private. More enthusiastic now, he kissed Mary, telling her he wanted to check in on Paul.

As he cycled back to the village, he wondered how Paul would great him today. He appeared to have turned a corner. Stuart knew he'd been taking new tablets; not everything worked, though. Conversations about school often caused him to revert to his shell. Stuart tried to imagine how it must feel to suffer a panic attack. He couldn't quite get his head around it. How terrible it must have been, he thought. No wonder Paul feared a return to school life. There had been talk of home schooling, though nobody had decided. Whatever would happen, Paul would find himself a long way behind in his studies, further adding to his pressure.

'Hi, how are you?' Stuart asked, surprised to see Paul out in the garden.

'Alright I suppose. Mum's insisting I keep busy if I'm staying off, so she's got me raking leaves. Waste of time if you ask me, but gets me out in the fresh air, right?'

Stuart chuckled. The smell in Paul's bedroom was definitely at odds with the garden.

'Come on,' Paul insisted. 'I've done my bit and you turning up earns me a break.'

The pair walked towards the back door, though Paul sulked as a sudden breeze lifted his leaf pile before dumping them back on the lawn.

'What's new?' Paul asked as he poured two glasses of cola and reached for a stash of crisps.

Stuart told him all about the plan for him to don a disguise and then accompany Mary and Bobbie to the school dance.

'No way. You're going to get your arse handed to you if you get caught.'

Stuart didn't need reminding. Already doubts had set in, though his desire to protect Mary meant he'd ignore them.

'Yeah, I know, but Mary means a lot to me and you know what some of them can be like.'

Paul winced.

Instantly, Stuart regretted his comment.

'Sorry. I know Harry and the others will be there and that worries me, if I'm honest. I could do with some backup.'

'You aren't suggesting I go to this thing, are you?'

'I won't force you. It's just I'm scared myself, you know, if Harry and the others turn up. I heard he's modelling himself on Bret Hart nowadays.'

Paul looked blank. The wrestler's name obviously meant nothing to him. It didn't matter, thought Stuart. He could see Paul was considering it.

'So you're going all made up as Dracula or someone?'

'I thought a werewolf if I can find a costume. Plenty of scope to keep my face hidden.'

Paul didn't offer any reply, but, as more days passed, Stuart found Paul asking more and more questions about the dance, what they would wear, how they'd sneak into the school.

Finally, with just one week to go, Paul agreed and in a meeting up at the farm, Paul, Stuart, Mary and Bobbie plotted to have the best teenage disco ever.

Chapter Twenty Eight

October 1983

SIMMONS STARED BLEAKLY AT the wall through eyes that sat in sunken sockets. He felt old and out of his depth. He glanced at a mirror before turning away in disgust. A mottled purple face had greeted him, showing his decline. Upon his desk lay piles of reports and tasks, which he refused to tackle. There would be a school inspection soon. Maybe that would be the final push, resulting in his departure. He deserved to go. Searching his mind, he sought a way out of the mess, but each time the haunting memories overwhelmed and he cowered within himself.

That morning, Mr Knowles had visited to whine about the upcoming Halloween disco. Christ, he'd been the teacher who'd begged for it to happen. Now the little shit announced he couldn't help run the sodding thing. Simmons considered his team of teachers and support staff. Where were they when he needed backing?

Arthur Morgan had also stepped through his door soon after. The curmudgeonly old caretaker's tirade had left Simmons shaken. Despite the old fart having a valid point regarding everyone's safety, the man had been abusive. Simmons had had no retort.

Daley had already bought a stash of gin and vodka. With the right encouragement, the kids were going to lap the booze up.

From the comfort of his flat, Daley counted ten bottles. The expense pained him, but it would be worth it if he could instigate a drunken riot where everyone would blame the head. And, if the free alcohol couldn't achieve his aim, Daley had other ways to bring about disaster. For now, though, Daley focussed on his first plan. Earlier that afternoon, he'd chosen two plastic containers. Each held a gallon, and he carefully decanted all the gin in one, the vodka in the other. Now to wait. He couldn't afford any witnesses when he delivered the booze.

As midnight approached, Daley stowed the two containers along with a metal one inside his Saab before driving quietly away. Even his headlights remained off until he turned out of his street. As expected, he didn't encounter any traffic. Daley knew the caretaker would have secured the gates, so all he could do at this stage would be to deliver the anonymous liquid to somewhere nearby. Dousing the car's lights a second time, Daley coasted the car until he could park in silence. Next, he removed all three canisters, grunting as the liquid sloshed about. Ahead lay tonight's goal.

A modern housing estate curved around half of the school boundary, and he shied away. His first step would be to locate a temporary store for the booze. The school had access to a running track which sat next to the playing fields, though getting there proved problematic. Being away from the homes helped, but squelching through deep mud along the way hampered his progress. Twice he lost a shoe, causing him to balance precariously before planting his sock-covered foot into the mire. He cursed under his breath. It took much longer than he wanted, especially as the three containers proved unwieldy. Eventually, however, he found the hut he was looking for and immediately set about unlocking the door. He peered into the inky interior. *Damn*. Before setting out on his covert mission, he had ruled out bringing a torch; that had been a mistake. From memory, he knew there would be a plethora of athletic equipment. With the summer over, most of the equipment would remain unattended. As his fingers reached into the dark, his knuckles hit something hard and he pulled back with a howl, dropping a canister. With clouds in the night sky and barely any moonlight, he wasn't sure what he'd hit. His fist stung. Tentatively this time, he found the fallen container and, once he'd set it upright, he nudged it behind the door where it sat alongside the other.

Securing the store, Daley angled across the playing fields to get closer to the school. He slipped upon the sodden grass; this time, he didn't sink. Nearing the tennis courts, he strode towards the outer edge, where he shoved the third canister. While the plastic gin and vodka containers were white, this one had a sludgy green colour. In the darkness, he wrapped the package in a dark cloth before shoving it towards the back of the hedge. Thorns added extra cuts to his hand, causing him to wince, but it would have to do. Tomorrow, once the school reopened, he would return and get the alcohol stashed inside.

'I don't know if I can do it.'

Stuart had expected this. 'I know, but remember what we said. I'm going along to support Mary and Bobbie, and you are there to support me. Come on, I'm really getting somewhere with Mary. I need you.'

Stuart immediately regretted manipulating his friend, though part of him realised Paul would have to get back into the world at some point. Maybe he was doing his friend a favour. Chancing his arm, Stuart applied a little more pressure.

'Do you remember Perez and Mohungu? Mary thinks if we brought them in, we'd be a strong enough unit to make Harry and the others think twice.'

Paul's face dropped. 'Those two won't want me there. I mean, why would they? They only know me as a bully.'

'You have a point. But they're good kids and given a choice between facing Harry's crew with you or without. I think they'd want you on their side. Plus, and I know you're going to hate this, when you broke down in class that time, those two looked really concerned. Mary told me they didn't laugh at seeing you like that. Shocked, maybe. They'll be okay.'

Stuart could see a glistening light appear in Paul's eyes. Maybe things would be alright.

Daley arrived at school early. He knew Arthur Morgan would unlock the gates by 7.30 a.m., giving him ample time before the arrival of other teachers and pupils. The only risk would be when he lugged two gallons worth of alcohol across the exposed playing fields.

Glad to see an early mist, he set off for the athletics shed. As he prised the door open, he saw a javelin with blood on it. He must have punched that last ight, he thought. Taking a tissue, Daley wiped the blood smears away, before looking forlornly at his own right hand.

Flexing his fingers hurt and he'd need a rational explanation for the injury, but he'd manage. Before anyone could disturb him, he pulled the two plastic bottles out from behind the door, which he locked after him.

By the time he'd returned to the school, Daley was sweating with his breath coming in heaves. *If only I was more fit,* he puffed, having trouble carrying the liquid across the playing fields. *At least I'm not in as bad a shape as Simmons*, he thought grimly, leaning against a wall to catch his breath before he finally stumbled inside. The building echoed his harsh breathing. There was no time to dwell. He had no explanation for why he was there or what he was carrying.

Knowing he only had a brief journey, Daley hefted the gin and vodka and set off along the corridor. At the end, he turned left to head to the rear of the stage, where he would hide the drinks. The door pushed inward, with him following. Immediately, Daley knew he wasn't alone. Somewhere nearby came a huffing sound. Daley closed the door silently and waited in the shadows.

Whoever it was, they were muttering and Daley froze. If they'd discover him, his plan threatened to be ruined. He *had* to succeed; had to set of a chain reaction of drunken pupils and a head, incompetent to deal with it. Frustrated, he waited, uncertainly. The noisy figure remained. Surely whoever it was, they must be on their way soon.

Daley considered his options. Heading back into the corridor held risks, so for now he stood his ground and hoped the intruder would move off into the main hall. Squinting, he could make out the time. It would soon be eight o'clock and teachers would arrive, ready for their day. As he looked across the back of the stage, he saw the storage lockers, tantalisingly out of reach. He'd give it another minute and then, if the figure remained, he'd have to abandon his plan. The seconds counted down with excruciating slowness, and Daley felt certain he'd need another hideaway, but just when he turned to leave, a thump sounded at the far end of the school hall.

'Oi. What are you doing in here?'

Daley recognised Arthur Morgan's voice. Upon hearing the caretaker, the intruder seemed to retreat, but the distraction afforded Daley the chance he needed. Breathing a sigh of relief and with his task accomplished, Daley disappeared back into the corridor. Within a few minutes, he'd left the school in readiness to drive back and arrive as normal.

Chapter Twenty Nine

WITH THE DISCO FAST approaching, Daley knew he still had one hurdle to overcome, and it would be risky. He felt sure his secret stash of alcohol was safe, but he needed to get enough kids stoned to cause trouble, and that wouldn't be easy. He certainly couldn't let anyone see him as the instigator.

A year earlier, he'd have trusted Paul as his co-conspirator. Daley felt troubled, thinking about his dalliance with the boy and how far Paul had fallen since. But he had more important things to deal with. Unable to figure a way around the problem, he grudgingly settled upon a conversation with Harry, trusting that the thug hated the school every bit as much as he did.

If his plan failed, he'd make sure the youngster took the fall, and if his plan worked and he'd become head, he'd expel Harry as soon as he could. The yob had such a reputation; he was sure his nefarious plan would work.

First, Daley discretely found all he could about the staffing arrangements for the night. The caretaker had already ruled himself out, saying he would lock up after but no more, and Knowles had withdrawn, leaving adult supervision decidedly light. Simmons had finally relented, saying he would be there. The thought excited Daley, spurring him on to engineer his boss' downfall. How wonderful it would be to see the bulbous waste of space come crashing down, with him ready to step into the void. In the end, there would be fewer than ten members of staff present to police the event. The only other adult representation came from outside the school: DJ Soundz, who'd rig the lights and run the music set.

Daley had made certain his name was absent from the list of staff attending. He would be there, of course, but had no intention of showing his face. Maybe, after the mayhem died down, he would appear, charging in with righteous indignation in the face of overwhelming evidence. *Yes, that could work*, he smiled.

It took two conversations with Harry to get him onboard. It irritated Daley that after the first chat, Harry left him hanging. He'd returned to his flat, feeling exasperated and more than vulnerable. He needn't have worried. Harry met with Daley soon after and together they started planning.

Around the hall and the stage were dark corners, tucked behind massive curtains which they would use. The school was providing soft drinks only; the cola, lemonade, and juice would serve brilliantly as mixers. Daley gave Harry a key to the store cupboard at the back of the stage. This would allow Harry, with the help of Eddie and Bruno, access to the alcohol.

Daley insisted they start off slowly, just pouring tiny measures into small groups until plenty of pupils felt the effects. He also cautioned against the know-it-all types who'd run for teacher support at the first sign of trouble. Harry was certain he could intimidate any troublemakers. Keen to make the drinking last as long as possible, they'd also agreed to separate the drinks to opposite sides of the stage. Then, if the worst happened, and they spotted the spiked drinks, they'd be able to continue serving them at the other side of the stage.

After sending Harry home, Daley poured himself a brandy. He considered the plan they'd made and was pleased, convinced it would work well. Deciding he needed a good long sleep, he disappeared off to bed. The following day was shaping up to be a busy one.

With Paul finally on board, Stuart felt relief, though under the surface he was a bag of nerves to sneak back into the school that had expelled him. It was too late to back out, so he'd just go with it and hope for the best.

Together with Paul, he walked up to the farm to meet Mary and Bobbie.

When Stuart walked into the kitchen, his eyes went wide. Across the table lay face paints, wigs, bandages and an array of makeshift costumes.

'Christ, Paul, you won't believe this.'

His friend almost fell through the doorway in surprise. Stuart chuckled as Paul tried on a clown mask.

'Hey, you don't need that. You're a clown already.'

'Yeah, yeah. Come on then, what are you going to wear?'

Before Stuart could answer, the girls came in. Mary looked sensational, as always, he thought. Even Bobbie looked amazing. Pulling Mary into a hug, he kissed, a move which always made his head spin. Then he released his girlfriend and gave Bobbie a peck on the cheek. Stepping back, he noticed Paul shy away. *A shame. It would have been nice to go on a double date*. Neither Mary nor Bobbie seemed to have noticed, so Stuart pushed any ideas of playing cupid aside to return to their preparation.

'Have we decided what everyone is wearing then?'

Mary rolled her eyes to convey he clearly hadn't been listening.

'What?'

Mary lifted a hairy costume and thrust it into his arms. Ah, the werewolf, he remembered.

'So that's me sorted, then. What about everyone else?'

Paul chose the bandages, allowing everyone to spend an hour wrapping him until only his eyes and mouth remained visible. Stuart felt some relief. His costume was stifling, though he could at least remove the hairy hood when things got too hot. Paul would suffer once they filed the hall along with lights and sweaty, gyrating teens.

Bobbie opted for a zombie. They spent half of the afternoon working on her make-up, resulting in a delightfully hideous creature.

That left Mary. Stuart looked on in excited anticipation. After applying a base layer of yellow around her cheeks and forehead, they switched colours to settle upon a dark shade of green. They all found applying her make-up hilarious and by the end, both Bobbies hands and part of her zombie outfit looked like she'd just climbed out from a swamp.

'How do I look?' Mary asked as Bobbie held a mirror tantalisingly out of reach.

Stuart marvelled, though he tried not to show it.

'Hand it over, will you?' Mary became impatient.

The others stood gawping, so Stuart reached over to prise the mirror from Bobbie's hands.

'There, happy now? Can you just accept you're going to steal the show, going dressed like that?'

Mary's jaw fell open as she moved the mirror in order to capture her reflection from every available angle.

'Come on, my wonderful witch, let's see you with your hat on. Yes, perfect. I just hope Dorothy and Toto don't turn up at the disco.'

Mary's smile broadened. She looked enchanting. Even Bobbie gasped before cheering, an action which breathed life into her zombie guise. Only Paul remained impassive, no surprise there as they'd bound him up. Instead, he gave a thumbs up and everyone cheered.

As they readied to walk back down to the village, from where Stuart's dad would drive them to the school, Stuart dashed back into the farmhouse. Seconds later, he returned clutching two drinking straws. Blank faces stared back.

'Look, I can't drink with this flipping mask across my head and neither can Paul, while you two can glug everything they put in front of you. We're going to get hot in there, at least carrying these, we two can sip a drink.'

'My boyfriend the genius,' Mary cheeked.

Stuart felt thrilled. Not only was he going to a dance with the most beautiful girl he knew, she called him her boyfriend *and* she thought he was a genius.

Chapter Thirty

Daley settled upon a grim reaper outfit. With a simple mask and dark hooded cloak, he knew he could move seamlessly within the school during the party. In his mind, he pictured a scythe hacking away at the idiot pupils who darkened his classroom every day. A cardboard crescent, wrapped in foil and attached to a broom handle, made for a poor substitute. It didn't matter. The wooden stave could still do some damage from the shadows.

Once again, he parked his Saab, only this time he settled for a dark side street, a short walk from the school. He wasn't about to head across the swamp-like field again. Once his car had halted away from any street lamps, Daley secured his mask in place and then he waited in darkness. The first delay came from young children. They only offered a minor threat, but their adult chaperones could remember his presence, so he sat quietly until they'd moved off to pester other households for treats. 'Beggars,' he muttered in disgusted irritation. At least the little bastards would find his flat empty tonight. He knew he didn't need to go to the school and he could leave everything to Harry and the others, but his ego and curiosity won. He had to see it. Besides, could he really trust Harry like he'd trusted Paul before?

At long last, the street appeared empty and Daley set off at a brisk pace. He avoided the main gates with the long driveway up to the school as parents drove up and down to deliver their offspring. Creeping behind the tennis courts, and using the black chain-link fence for cover, he retrieved the metal canister he'd stashed the night before. He hoped its contents wouldn't be necessary.

With music blaring in the distance and everyone focussing on getting to the entrance, his progress went unchecked. As he neared the staff parking area, he allowed himself a little smile. Simmons' car sat there with four pristine tyres as a tempting target. Reluctantly, he passed on by, choosing merely to spit in contempt upon the vehicle. Muddying the water by vandalising the head's car a second time served no purpose. The gym offered private entry into the school. He knew the door should be unlocked as the school wanted additional fire exits while the disco ran, but it came as a relief when it opened all the same. The night felt cold and Daley's breath eerily formed plumes which dissipated in the darkness.

Nobody saw him as he entered the school.

'Thanks, Dad,' Stuart said as he climbed into the front passenger seat while clutching Mary's hat. The other three friends squeezed into the rear of the family Austin Allegro, with Paul grumbling the most. Stuart understood. He was already overheating in his own costume, but for the moment, he could take his head mask off and lay it on the floor. Winding the window down helped as they drove the miles into school.

His parents hadn't been too keen at first, when they heard of Stuart's resolve to go to the party but his motive, protecting Mary, had won them over. It came as a relief, especially since his dad had offered to drive them and collect them later that evening.

As soon as they arrived at the school, everyone clambered out into the cold and the car pulled away. Up ahead, the school took on a foreboding air as an autumn mist clung. Cars, parents and pupils seemed to swarm about, forcing Stuart to don the mask which covered his head. For now, while outside, he appreciated the warmth the hood offered; inside would be different.

While mucking about in the farmhouse, his werewolf outfit had seemed a brilliant idea. Now, doubts surfaced. He couldn't hear properly, everything was muffled and his vision was impaired as well. Stuart gripped Mary's hand tightly, not only to support her, but also for guidance.

Someone must have said something, as Mary's arm jerked and he stumbled along. If need be, Stuart would lift the mask to see properly. *I should have darkened my face with make-up*, he thought.

The noise sounded much louder now as they approached the school hall, echoing with a dull bass beat to a tune Stuart didn't recognise. As the crowd swelled, Stuart's anxiety heightened. He was sure Paul felt the same. He hoped they'd stick together and see the party through. A queue formed, forcing the group into a sandwich, while they waited in line. The process seemed inexplicably slow, though eventually they moved forward. Mary squeezed his hand, offering reassurance.

Soon, they would encounter the first hurdle. Around him a multitude of voices, all clamouring to be heard above the music inside. And then, they were there, at the head of the queue, having their tickets inspected. Stuart braced himself, but the check was quick and their fake names weren't arousing suspicion.

They were inside. The group swept left away from everyone, shoving their way in until they found some space. Stuart faced towards the wall and lifted his mask to study the room properly. The hall appeared to be half full of students; he couldn't make out any teachers. He should have felt relief, but the thought the staff was watching from the shadows, supervising, made him nervous.

Once he'd completed his scan of the room, he could see they were in a relatively safe space. Near to the stage, someone had cobbled together a basic lighting rig. A solitary disco ball spun idly while three coloured spotlights alternated between white, red and green. At their end, the lighting worsened, with only green fire exit signs offering illumination. A few metres further along the wall, Stuart noticed Hugo Perez and Jonny Mohungu.

Neither boy seemed to have received the memo explaining the Halloween theme. Hugo wore a white shirt with a salmon pink tie and dark trousers, while Jonny had chosen jeans paired with a denim top. With a riot of costumes, ranging from dreadful through to amazing, the pair cringed disconsolately. Jonny was looking down, while Hugo merely looked embarrassed.

'Come on, let's go chat with Jonny and Hugo. They look so downcast without a costume and I think we'd all feel better in a bigger group of friends.'

Daley closed the outer door and looked across the gymnasium through squinted eyes. At ceiling height sat a row of windows, though little light filtered through and Daley wondered whether he was alone. Some crappy pop song played with a muted throb, further hampering his effort to listen to others. No, he was certain nobody would be down here. Not tonight.

Taking a few tentative steps, his confidence grew. Even though the wooden floor echoed his walk, the distant beat of the music cancelled everything out so someone would have to be up close before detecting him. Still, he couldn't afford complacency. Reaching the opposite end, he used the wall for guidance to move along until he located the door. Daley checked he'd secured his mask in place before nudging it open. He didn't expect to find anyone outside, though, knowing kids and their proclivity for mischief, he had to remain careful. The outer room, which had no windows, remained in darkness. He flicked on the light switch. A glimmer of light shone beneath the furthest door, out into the corridor, but Daley considered the risk worthwhile as his eyes fought to adjust to the new glare.

He removed his mask and inhaled deeply, with closed eyes, savouring the sweaty aroma which stemmed from a box of garments labelled "lost property". It amused him how pupils would forget their PE kit and then look on in horror at being told to wear something from the box. Daley would have loved to thrust his nose into the clothing and breathe in the odour of teenage adolescence, but tonight he had to focus.

To the right lay the changing rooms, all empty and clean, with no showering youths to entice him. To his left lay an office. Barry Potts, the head of PE, claimed the room belonged to him. Daley tried the door and, finding it locked, he stepped away. It didn't matter. The sweaty clothing mound offered an ideal hiding place for the can. Decision made, he buried the object underneath. After carefully checking he'd left no clues, Daley, shrouded in his grim reaper outfit, doused the lights once more. This time he exited into a dim corridor, which would lead him along to the back of the stage, where he could lurk and intervene if needed.

Using Mary with her tall hat for cover, Stuart lifted his mask almost entirely off his head. At last, he could breathe properly, he thought, even if it would only be for a short time. A trickle of sweat wandered across his brow, reminding him Paul was suffering more than any of them. Wiping his furry arm across his head, he turned to his former classmates.

'Hi, Jonny, and Hugo,' he beamed.

'Whoa. Stuart, is that you?' Jonny exclaimed.

'Sure is. Mary wants to pull some moves on the dancefloor and I just had to come along for that.'

'Wow. We didn't expect to see you, but it's great you're here.'

Hugo nodded in agreement. Stuart watched as Jonny's eyes panned from him, to Mary, then to Bobbie, before finally settling upon Paul. He frowned. 'Is that...?'

Stuart nodded, pulling Paul closer. 'Yes, it's Paul. I know what you're both thinking,' he shouted above the noise, 'but it's ok. Paul isn't who he used to be; he really has changed. Obviously, we'd like to keep it secret that he's here, hence the bandages.'

Both Jonny and Hugo looked troubled. They offered tentative nods, but it was clear they weren't too happy about Paul's presence. It didn't matter to Stuart. He knew they would help if any trouble would come their way, so Stuart felt safe in their presence.

Seeing the dancefloor fill up, Bobbie grabbed Mary to pull her into the throng. The DJ had just launched into "Down Under" by Men at Work, which galvanised most of the girls, while the boys looked on grimacing sheepishly. Too afraid to join in, Stuart grinned. His face fell. He hadn't told Mary he hated dancing. He considered himself clumsy, and hoped his girlfriend would not notice. Placing his rubber mask back over his head, he groaned. Earlier, when they'd dressed, they'd done so with bright lights, but now Stuart faced an uncomfortable choice. If he stayed in the shadows, he could safely remove part of his disguise, but Mary wouldn't accept that. Some knight in shining armour he'd be, watching from the sidelines. No, he would have to dance, but Mary would need to lead him through the crowd until they found a brighter part of the room for him to have any chance of seeing his surroundings. The idea filled him with dread.

Stuart pushed through a sea of costumes. If Mary hadn't worn her tall hat, he would have missed her, but at last he gripped her hand and pulled her towards the delicate dots of light created by a solitary disco ball near the stage. As the song ended, he cringed inside the suit. *Not "Flashdance"!* Around them, kids bounced and buffeted, adding to his discomfort. He tried his best, but he knew he couldn't keep up with the tempo and twice, he came close to stamping on Mary's toes. In the end, Bobbie stepped in and the three held on in some bizarre triangular line dance.

While the songs continued to play, Stuart became caught up with the two girls. Had he considered Paul, he'd have realised his friend had unravelled all the bandages around his head to breathe properly. Now, only the shadows would keep Paul from being seen.

Daley finally found the vantage point he wanted. Standing in the darkness, he had an extra layer of protection behind a stage curtain and he remained behind the DJ, who continued to assault his eardrums with a dreadful cacophony of tracks. He supposed it didn't matter as long as these were the songs the kids liked. So far, he'd spotted Harry across one side of the hall. Before the dance, they'd agreed he should wear a Frankenstein mask. Daley could make out several, though only one with Harry's muscular forearms. The thug seemed to be in a perfect spot, within easy reach of a table containing soft drinks. Now and then, one of his colleagues would pop along in a half-hearted attempt at supervision, though their actions seemed lacklustre. Daley knew why. Most staff hated Simmons and now he'd forced them into working extra hours for the party. They lacked the enthusiasm to behave professionally. Every time the cola and squash lay unattended, he saw Harry sweep down to grab a few cups. Squinting in the darkness, Daley saw Eddie and Bruno. He shook his head at their costumes. Both boys wanted to dress up as ghouls, though to Daley they looked more like two upright pillowcases after a fight.

Finally, the boys created a system which seemed to adhere to Daley's plan. With Harry at one side and Eddie and Bruno at the other, the boys were conducting an illicit trade in spiked drinks, right underneath everyone's nose. As long as they didn't rush things, his plan could work.

Occasionally, some kids would jump up onto the stage to talk to the DJ. Each time Daley shook with rage, as their incursion could easily draw attention to him or the others. Feverishly, he clutched the curtain rather than lash out with his wooden stave. They wouldn't notice a crying kid immediately, but eventually an adult would come. Daley held back reluctantly, though he made a note of their faces, so he could seek retribution later.

Then, as one song ended, Daley saw a door open at the far end of the hall. Bright light yawed in and there was no mistaking the head's chubby form. The man just stood there while the DJ mucked about with his next song choice. People didn't seem to notice, despite the new dazzle cast upon them. This was the first time that evening Daley had properly noticed the far end of the hall, which earlier had sat in shadow. Wretched pupils, jiggling in their stupid prancing, met his gaze. His scrutiny continued as he sought more members of staff, when suddenly his panning head stopped. It couldn't be, could it? Simmons closed the door, plunging that section of the hall back into darkness. And with that, the image of Paul, wrapped in some weird bandage garb, disappeared.

The appearance left Daley feeling uncertain.

Chapter Thirty One

SIMMONS CURSED UNDER HIS breath, though once the music started up again, it would have hardly mattered if he'd sworn out loud. Where were they, his bloody staff? The disco could turn into a disaster if they didn't step up to supervise. He considered if this was his fate. After seeing Emily in the park, he wondered whether that was the signal karma would come to collect.

Grumbling, he marched diagonally through the dancers, most of whom bounced off his engorged frame while barely registering the head. With his progress halted by a pantomime horse, he switched right and finally, broke through the perimeter and found the entrance. A trickle of newcomers continued, though it looked as though everyone who planned to come had already arrived.

Seeing Ned Fairclough came as a relief. At least one teacher hadn't turned against him. Deciding any latecomers were out of luck, he sent Ned back into the hall with instructions to roam about and keep order. Once alone, Simmons set about securing the door.

As he returned to the hall and from there his office, he felt a pang of guilt. This was high school, with him in charge, and yet he could draw little recognition from the faces scattered out before him. Obviously, the masks, movement and poor lighting were a factor, but Simmons still felt a sense of disconnect. He would have to do better. Then, perhaps more people would be on his side and he could make some kind of positive legacy.

Deciding he could do little by remaining in his office, Simmons returned the way he came. This time, he moved judiciously around the edge of the room. Once again, light flooded one end of the hall and, in a rare show of grace, he studied his pupils. Many wore haphazard outfits, better suited to a jumble sale. A few had made a genuine effort. Even the odd pantomime horse he'd seen earlier offered a weird charm, though he wouldn't describe it as scary. An odd thought crossed his mind as his eyes caught sight of a figure wearing bandages which seemed to unravel across the floor. Simmons felt sure he should know the boy. As he left to head back to the offices, he hoped recognition would come to him.

Daley felt conflicted. He was there to supervise Harry and the other two from the shadows, to make certain as many pupils would fall into a drunken melee as possible, but months had gone by with little news. Surely, he could approach Paul undetected.

The kids packed the front of the dancefloor and as far as Daley could tell, plenty of students seemed a little drunk. Either that, or they were hopeless at dancing. From the shadows, Harry, Eddie and Bruno continued their discrete distribution. Daley just had to hope they'd continue uninterrupted. Trusting Harry knew what to do once a few kids became too drunk, Daley disappeared back into the deserted corridor. From here, he could run parallel to the hall and up towards the offices. He wouldn't go that far, as several glass doors would allow easy access to the hall. He counted to six before stopping to find out where Paul could be. With his mask back in place and scythe in hand, he entered the hall once more. Here the bedlam seemed worse, as kids of all sized bounced around with gleeful disregard for anyone around them. Daley could knock them about a bit with impunity.

Casting a menacing figure, Daley moved through the crowd, keen to see whether he *had* seen Paul. At first, it appeared hopeless. There were just too many irritating children. Then, Daley remembered the doorway Simmons had used earlier. He wouldn't want to see the head, but with the bright lights behind, he'd take a chance.

Slowly he turned the handle, allowing the outer hall lights to blaze through. Seeing it empty, Daley turned his attention back to the search for Paul. Immediately, he struck gold. He had been right. There he was, hunched over in the corner with two other boys. Daley studied the three, before closing the door and returning them all to the Halloween gloom. The three seemed to be together. Daley didn't want witnesses, but he desperately needed to talk to Paul. He had nudged himself a few metres along the wall, looking for an opportunity, when Simmons returned. Again, the bright outer hall illuminated the area and Daley cowered, afraid to be recognised.

Simmons' cogs had turned until he remembered who the boy was. Paul something, he recalled. The lad had taken a funny turn over the summer and hadn't been back to school since. Ordinarily he would have discounted the idea, but today Simmons wanted to show his more compassionate side, show the pupils he cared.

Searching the hall, he found the noise and movement overwhelming once the door closed behind him; he wondered how he could find anyone. He opened the door through which he'd come a bit. The light would help.

The DJ started playing Spandau Ballet's "True". He smiled, glad to recognise one song at least. Maybe he wasn't an old duffer after all. Mouthing the words, he moved about the hall, looking for telltale bandages.

Paul looked about uncomfortably. Why had he agreed to come to the disco? Bobbie, Mary and Stuart all appeared to be enjoying themselves, but where did that leave him? He looked across at Jonny and Hugo, sitting on the sidelines, engrossed in a Rubik's cube neither would ever finish. One word sat heavy in his mind, *alone*.

He stood, not caring who saw, and felt eyes burning on him. A few metres away, someone dressed as the Grim Reaper stood watching. The monstrous creature returned his stare. Paul shivered. Somehow, he didn't think it was a pupil. That left the staff and suddenly, he knew exactly who was staring at him with eyes which drilled into the darkest recesses of his soul. An old fear returned, his hands started shaking. This couldn't happen again.

Abruptly, he shoved off along the wall, knocking Jonny into the progress. He didn't hear the protest as the colourful puzzle clattered across the floor; he didn't hear half the school belting out Gary Kemp's lyrics. It was all he could do to lumber across the floor towards an exit. He *had* to get out.

Disorientated, he gripped a handle. Relief flooded over him as the door swung open. A gloomy corridor beckoned, lit only by emergency exit signs. He knew where he was, though he didn't want to be here, not this side of the school. Ahead lay the changing rooms, along with a horrific memory etched in his mind. The rational thing would be to turn about and head up towards the offices. Up there would be light and a safe passage out of the building, but one thing stopped him. Teachers, pupils, anyone could be there. He just couldn't do it. Not another collapse with hoards of people looking on. Their laughter would ring in his ears forever. Instead, haunted by other, darker memories, Paul sped off towards the darkened gymnasium.

When he finally reached the door leading towards the gym, it opened to an oppressive darkness. He stopped. He didn't want to enter, but could he really turn around?

The doorhandle felt cold and slick. Paul looked down with glossy confused eyes as he tried to control his shaking fingers. He released the handle, kept the door ajar with his knee. All he needed was a little time to get his head together. He should have foreseen Daley's presence. Why hadn't he thought of it before? Paul's forehead drummed gently against the doorframe while he processed everything. A small part of him desperately wanted to go back. At least up there he had Stuart, Mary and Bobbie and maybe even the other two. But then, they'd gone off to dance and left him stewing in his own mire of neurosis. He started crying.

It was then that he heard it, a distant voice, distorted by the music within the hall. Someone was calling his name. He shook his head to work out who it was. Several eery seconds passed while he waited, then the call came again, louder, clearer.

Paul shuddered. He recognised the voice. A deep unease wrapped tightly around his torso until breathing became difficult. Slowly, he sank into darkness.

Chapter Thirty Two

Stuart needed a rest. He considered himself fit, but the costume, when combined with dancing, had worn him out.

'How many songs was that?' he asked breathlessly.

'What?' Mary replied.

Stuart lifted the mask off his head. He didn't want to be spotted, but his desire to breathe properly overrode his misgivings.

'Sorry,' he said a little louder. 'Flipping heck, that was fun. How many songs did we dance to?'

'Not enough,' Mary teased, though she, too, looked ready for a breather.

The two of them and Bobbie moved through the crowd until they spied Jonny and Hugo. This time, their progress was unhampered. It seemed a few others needed a break too, and with light streaming in from the far end, they found their friends easily.

'Hey, guys. Where's Paul?' Stuart shouted.

The pair looked startled.

Hugo spoke, 'He left.'

Crap, thought Stuart guiltily. He should have kept an eye on his friend.

'He was here a minute ago though,' Jonny offered, pointing the way.

Pulling Mary and Bobbie closer, Stuart suggested they come along, telling Jonny and Hugo to follow if they weren't back in ten minutes. The three set off for the corridor.

Simmons was sure he'd seen Paul leave, but it took over a minute to cross the hall owing to an influx of dancers who sprang up for Laura Branigan's "Gloria". At last, he turned a handle and pushed through to the gloomy corridor behind. He closed the door and strained both ears, but couldn't hear a sound.

Having come from the offices earlier, Simmons assumed Paul must have gone towards the gymnasium. It wouldn't take long to check, he thought, and lumbered off into the darkness.

Before they could leave the hall, an angry shout erupted, causing Stuart to skid to a halt.

'Oi. I know you. What are you doing here? You shouldn't be in our school.'

Stuart looked about in panic as he sought the person who'd called him out. It was too late for him to place his werewolf mask back over his head. After several fruitless seconds, he spotted the owner of the voice. Whether it was the mask, or the build of the speaker, Stuart couldn't be sure, but something caused an involuntary shudder.

'I'm allowed here for the disco,' he responded, trying to sound confident. 'Anyway, who are you to say, whether I'm allowed here? You're not in charge.'

The person stepped forward, though each step seemed laboured somehow. Then the figure stopped. With their exit blocked, a confrontation seemed inevitable. Buoyed by Mary and Bobbie, Stuart tried again.

'Who are you?'

As the figure reached up a solid forearm to remove the mask, Stuart's heart sank. It was Harry. The bully's grin paired with eyes which glistened with malice.

'I'm going to have some fun. It's about time someone gave you a proper kicking,' he slurred.

Stuart cursed again. Where were the sodding teachers? He felt a squeeze in his hand as Mary drew alongside, with Bobbie following suit. The gesture helped, but he couldn't let them fight his battle. Harry stepped closer, and Stuart braced himself for a punch. It never came.

From nowhere came a flash of pink as Hugo surged forward. An object thudded hard into Harry's jaw. The dancers continued as they had done all night; Stuart and the others looked on in stunned admiration. Harry howled, clutching his face before toppling backwards. A second later, Jonny arrived. Together with Hugo, they searched the floor, while Harry curled into a ball and whimpered. They soon found the Rubik's cube, which Hugo waved triumphantly.

Stuart grinned widely. 'Thanks, you two! I couldn't have tackled him on my own.'

Hugo and Jonny smiled as Stuart set off into the corridor once more in his search for Paul.

'Come on Paul. Where are you? I know you're down here. I just want to talk,' pleaded Daley. He needed to understand what had gone wrong between them both. Paul shouldn't fear him, not after all the intimacy they'd shared.

Daley arrived at the end of the corridor and, after checking the toilets, he returned to the room he'd been in earlier. The door opened silently, but even to Daley, the oppressive darkness felt uninviting. He called Paul's name once again, softer this time. Now they were away from the disco beat. When he heard no response, he leaned in to click the light switch. The room remained exactly as before. He strode into the showers, but before he could check them properly, he heard a noise. The noise didn't seem human, as a soft mewing sound caught his ear. He spun about. If it came from Paul, he knew where to go.

Paul blinked repeatedly when the gym lights erupted around him. Immediately, he curled his head downwards as his body backed into the corner.

'There you are. I knew it was you in the hall.'

Paul knew the voice, but he couldn't bring himself to look up. Instead, the ball knotted inside his stomach tightened, mirroring his body pose. The shaking returned, only now the tremor had intensified as his entire torso quivered in fear. An arm, unexpected and unwanted, reached across his shoulders. He couldn't cope with the intrusion and both arms shoved back hard.

Daley must have knelt as now he tumbled backward and the two stared at one another for the first time in months. All Paul could see was a stranger.

'Don't be like that. Come on, Paul. Surely you remember how special you are to me?'

What did he mean? Paul was confused. Months of self-isolating torment had convinced him Daley had used him all along.

'Get away from me,' he uttered feebly.

Suddenly, Daley's demeanour changed. His outer facade disappeared, showing a menace and cruelty instead. Paul winced as his teacher grabbed his arm in an iron grip, forcing him to stand. Then a shove came. A dull thud echoed as his head hit the wall. He pushed back. Daley briefly faltered, allowing Paul to duck underneath his grasping arms.

He screamed with all the power of his pent-up agony. 'You're off your head, you sicko. We're done here. Nobody will allow you to teach when I tell them what you did to me. They're going to lock you up.'

He *had* to get away. He saw the house of sand he'd built with Daley had been an illusion. Suddenly, he understood everything. The confused feelings, the experimentation, all of it, led and controlled by his teacher. Paul shook his head. Things seemed clearer now after months of muddled thoughts. He turned away, though only managed one step before Daley set upon him.

'Who the fuck do you think you're talking to? I looked after you, you little bastard. I cared for you and this is how you repay me. You threaten me.'

Paul stumbled as Daley lashed out. A boot landed behind his knee and Paul collapsed in agony. As he writhed, more blows landed.

'You must think I'm fucking stupid if you think you can bring me down. Do you want to know what happened last time? I smashed her fucking face into the road, that's what. She wanted to tell everyone. She said she knew my dirty little secret. Here, let me show you just what I did to her.'

Paul screamed as Daley gripped his hair, lifted his head and pushed it forcibly forward. Again and again. After the third time, Daley stopped. Paul lay immobile, fearing what more was to come. He couldn't get up, and his right eye was closed, his left still worked. He saw Daley leave but the relief was short-lived.

The teacher returned seconds later, clutching a canister in one hand, shaking it. Paul's one good eye widened in horror. He tried to move; he *had* to move, but his body refused to cooperate. All he could do was watch the scene unfold.

Daley hovered over him. He grinned inanely as he pointed to the canister.

'See what you've done? You made me do this. I wanted to fix everything, but you, you threatened me and now you're going to burn.'

For the fourth time, Daley smashed Paul's face into the floor and this time, perhaps mercifully, Paul's left eye did not reopen.

Simmons spotted the light flare from underneath the door with growing optimism. Surely, his quest to find Paul was at an end. Pushing through, he saw nobody, but before he could check the changing rooms, he heard a thud. Reaching the door to the gym, he detected an unusual smell and instantly knew something was wrong. He burst through. Nothing could have prepared him for that moment. He'd found the boy he'd been looking for in a crumpled mess on the floor, his costume's white linen ribbons bloodstained.

To the boy's left stood Daley, unrecognisable. A pair of dark malevolent eyes stared at him from beneath a hood. Simmons stepped forward, and then, as he realised Daley's intent, he stopped short.

'Why?'

Daley let loose a guttural grown and charged. Simmons saw with dread he would be the next victim if he didn't act fast. Desperately he sought a way out. The door seemed too far away. He knew he wasn't fit enough to run away. That left only one option. He'd have to fight. Daley leaped towards him, wielding a metal object, just as Simmons moved. He got lucky and Daley sailed past him to plop on the floor. There, near the boy, he could see something, a weapon maybe? Clutching his chest, Simmons rushed over. He had no time to inspect Paul, as Daley would be upon him in an instant, but he grabbed Daley's makeshift scythe, the wooden staff. He turned to parry Daley's attack. His first hit landed and Daley staggered backwards, clutching his ribs. In one movement, he'd recovered enough to swing a canister. It sloshed liquid as it sailed through the air.

Simmons braced, but the object was heavier than he imagined and he fell to the floor. As he lay panting and defenceless, Simmons understood exactly what was in the cannister. Terrified, he saw petrol pooled around the floor and across his suit.

Seeing his prone form, Daley stood and laughed. 'You should have stayed away. Neither of you needed to be here. You asked me why. I guess I can tell you now you're about to go up in flames. He was going to tell everyone about our relationship. I couldn't let that happen. Not again. I had to shut him up, just like the last one.'

Daley laughed maniacally.

'This is brilliant, you know. I've wanted your job for years. Oh, how I've watched you squirm as you dealt with the notes I sent. And when you sacked Una Tavistock, I looked on as your mistakes piled up. I must congratulate you upon coming here tonight, Mr Simmons, *former* head of the school. Don't you see? You've come here tonight. It's fate. I wanted rid of you and now you're here, offering yourself up as a sacrificial lamb.'

And then Simmons knew with unerring certainty. The wretched feeling he'd carried for years intensified as he realised everything Daley had done. It didn't matter. While his pupils all danced the night away, just a few metres along a corridor, he would lie in torment, unable to stop the monster who'd taught in his school for years. Everything had come full circle and now, Simmons felt empty. Perhaps this was justice, after all. He had lead Emily to believe they had a future and then failed her after she was assaulted. Just when she needed him most, he'd abandoned her. Surely, he deserved this ending. Looking over, he saw Paul, lain out in a twisted mess and his sorrow deepened.

Daley laughed once more before limping over to retrieve the petrol can. All the while, Simmons slumped. It was the flame that triggered him into action. Daley held the lighter aloft while slowly spinning to take in the scene as though offering one last macabre farewell. Any thought of self-preservation had gone, but in a desperate last act to save Paul, Simmons launched with everything he had. Gripping the staff, he piled into Daley, knocking him down.

As they tussled, the lighter slipped out of Daley's hand. The Zippo skidded across the wooden floor and for the briefest of moments, Simmons thought he'd won.

Then the inferno erupted.

Stuart thundered down the corridor with the others close behind when the first scream sounded. He dived through the door into a world of smoke and chaos. Immediately, he appraised the situation. Two smouldering bodies writhed in some hellish battle. From the build, he guessed one was Simmons, and he wondered what to do.

Then he saw Paul, laying still, perilously close to the flames, which edged ever closer.

The heat intensified as a river of flame shot up, blocking his path. Coughing, Stuart wrapped his furry mask across his mouth and ran. He couldn't save the two, but he could get to Paul.

'Come on, help me,' he shouted as the others entered the gym. Together, they dashed forward, leaping away from flames as they ran. It took a momentous effort to pull Paul clear, and once they'd retreated outside the gym, there would be no going back. For a few seconds, screams echoed about the room before falling silent.

Nobody else would come out of the school gymnasium alive.

Christmas 1983

'How is she?'

'Oh, you know. She's mum. Nothing much changes. Maybe one day she'll come back to us.'

Stuart patted Emily's hand. As expected, he didn't receive a reaction, though on other days, something did register. Satisfied he'd said hello properly, he turned to plant a kiss on Mary's lips.

'That's better. Thank you. I've been wanting to do that since I woke up this morning. Didn't you see the mistletoe over the door?'

'Have you indeed? Well, I'm glad you did. Let's share another one,' he winked.

They kissed hungrily before Stuart broke away.

'Paul's heading over later. He seems a lot steadier this week.'

'That's good. I'm glad he's talking about stuff more. Bobbie said she would visit too. I foresee a makeover session and lots of dancing ahead, especially as you've improved since our first dance.'

Stuart took her compliment with good grace while marvelling at how, only two months on, they could talk about that night. Paul's physical recovery had been swift; emotionally, they all knew things would take a lot longer. The doctors reckoned the springy gym floor had just enough give to limit any lasting damage. The surface was certainly softer than any tarmac.

The school had lost its head teacher, along with Mr Daley plus the gymnasium remained gutted, but beyond that only Harry, with a lost tooth, had been injured. Firefighters had arrived quickly before the flames could spread and once the ashes lay cold, the truth as told by Paul came out. There were other victims, like Molly Simmons. The head's part in the fire remained clouded, though Paul's story offered the man some redemption, by suggesting he at least had tried to stop Daley's attempt at murder.

The police would look at Emily's cold case, they all knew that, but with Daley turned into a smouldering corpse, they would want to close the book soon so the family could move on in peace. They all knew Paul hadn't been Daley's first, and maybe, somewhere, there was a man or even men haunted by their past. Unless someone came forward, their stories would remain untold.

'It's a shame Paul and Bobbie won't ever get together,' Mary mused.

'Maybe, but it doesn't matter, does it? Somewhere is the right person for Bobbie and the right man for Paul. They're our friends and I'm okay with that.'

'Quite right,' she smiled, 'Now, how about another kiss?'

Acknowledgements

I would like to thank Caroline, and everyone else at City Stone Publishing for all their efforts with the publication of this book. It means a lot for me to work with you.

For thanks, I want to single out my wife. You have kindness at your core and I'm immensely lucky to share my life with you.

More thanks must also go to Kim Rigby, Nicki Murphy, Geoff Worsley, and Fran Wilson Vaughan, as well as everyone who followed the development of this novel. Your encouragement helped a lot.

And finally, a thank you, to you, my readers, for purchasing this book. I hope you enjoyed the story enough to tell your friends and family and that you'll look out for my future works. I'd love it if you could take the time to submit a review with the vendor you bought the book from as this really helps.

Alistair Birch

www.alistairbirch.com
Sign up for my newsletter: www.alistairbirch.com/sign-up/

About the Author

Alistair Birch is the author of two modern action-packed thrillers, *Shadow Pursuit* and the sequel *Shadow Play* and the character driven psychological coming-of-age novel, *The Evil Within*.

Not content to stop there, Alistair is currently writing a wartime thriller while considering another Shadow book and other writing projects.

Outside of the writing world, Alistair combines another job role in IT; friends often see him running around his hometown in south Oxfordshire before signing up for the occasional distance race.

He loves cooking and has a cheeky side which transfers to silly rhymes, some of which he's published in his own collection.

Alistair Birch's website: www.alistairbirch.com
Facebook Author Page: facebook.com/alistairbirchauthor
Twitter: @ABirchAuthor

About City Stone Publishing

Publisher with a passion for the written word and a heart that beats for our authors

We are an imaginative and enthusiastic indie publisher.

Our ambition is twofold:

To develop outstanding books and work alongside our authors.

To be a beacon of advice and a provider of services for indie authors.

We are not just about the books; we build relationships with our authors. Because we both write, we know what (indie) authors want. That is how we work: in cooperation and partnership with our authors.

From dark and gritty crime thrillers, adventurous fantasy, entertaining women's fiction, and intriguing contemporary novels to interesting and insightful non-fiction and visionary poetry, we publish it all.

Visit our website: citystonepublishing.com

Printed in Great Britain
by Amazon

24333306R00138